THE WARLORD'S QUEEN

J.E. & M. KEEP

DEDICATION

To our friends who didn't judge, readers of The Keep back when we were first starting out, and Darknest Fantasy Erotica who encouraged us to keep going.

THE WARLORD'S QUEEN

CONTENTS

CONTENT WARNING

J.E. & M. Keep recognize that erotica can be very personal, and that everyone has their limits on what they wish to read. Because of this, we provide content warnings for all our erotica so that you can avoid any **triggering material** – or find the story you most want to read. If you want your book spoiler free, please skip this section!

This particular story contains non-monogamy, Dominant / submissive roles, and difficult pregnancy.

CHAPTER 1

A city of ancient glory and grandeur, Ariste burned far below in a deservingly splendid way. Even in its death throes, it was magnificent, the Princess thought.

Though none of that stopped the tears from flowing.

She was not yet officially come of age. The ceremony was planned for her engagement when the southern Prince arrived come the summer. It was long ago determined, and even the commoners knew of it—a continuation of the political alliance that kept the city-state of Ariste aligned with the sprawling Empire that vastly dwarfed it.

Aligned, but separate.

So young. Still oh-so delicate, but facing the worst tragedy in the many millennia of her royal line.

If the armies of the northern hordes were upon her doorstep, then it could mean only one thing: her father's military expedition had failed. And he was dead. Though her own young life was what struck her most poignantly. It was soon to be over, was it not? As she watched dark shadows move through the fiery streets below, laying waste to ancient artistry in the stonework, she wondered what there could be to live for.

Even should some hero sweep in and rescue her, all that she was to inherit, all that she ever lived for, would be gone or spoiled. Ariste would be a shell.

She thought then of flinging herself from her balcony, and her slender, pale fingers worked the latch of her double-door, taking light steps outside. Though she was so far above the din, the roar of flame and savage voices still carried up to her. It was worse than the harvest festival.

Her fingers trailed along the marble railing, and as if in a sleepy daze, she grasped hold, her shaking hands suddenly steady. She knew what she had to do.

She began to climb up onto the railing, lifting one leg, when the door to her room rudely opened in a sudden jerk and she cried out in shock.

"Princess!" Mirella's voice called out, the older servant looking alarmed but collected. She'd been property of the royal family for many long years, taking care of Princess Anabelle since she was but a babe. And her presence brought calm and doubt back to the young woman's heart.

How could she fling herself to her doom when still at least one of her closest still remained?

"Get down, they're coming! They're in the castle," Mirella urged, the servant rushing over to her and helping her away from the railing and back into the manor.

Mirella. Her saviour.

Traitor.

CHAPTER 2

Mirella awoke with a start. Her heart was pounding, her ivory skin dewy with perspiration. Even after the months of inhabiting her new body, it was still so odd to her. In the faint moonlight that trailed in through the window, her delicate skin seemed almost luminescent.

Younger, smaller, more delicate. All things that Mirella had never thought she would or could be. And what had it taken?

Betraying the girl you helped raise.

She brushed back her golden hair, wiped away the sweat from her brow, and leaned back on the many opulent pillows. She'd tricked the Princess into switching bodies with her to win her escape. And she'd done that, but Mirella had no intention of going back.

The Princess had been taken away from Ariste, where she was put on trial and charged as a traitor elsewhere for Mirella's crimes. In the Empire.

Mirella, now Queen of Ariste, dismissed the unbidden thoughts. She may have done more to raise Anabelle than anyone, but it wasn't by choice. It was slavery. *I was property*, she reminded herself. *And if I cunningly turned the tables, it was just deserts.*

Her stomach twinged, and she was reminded of the life that stirred within her. She wore only a gossamer night gown that cupped her swollen breasts and accomplished little else. The see-through fabric fanned out around her round, pregnant belly, the one round area on her otherwise dainty body. She cradled it, and for a moment thought of her first child. The child she'd birthed in the body of Mirella.

He was hers, but officially only by adoption. The God-King Kulav was his father, of that there was no doubt, but only a select few knew that Mirella had switched bodies with the Princess. How would she explain that to her son?

Her mind burned with countless different thoughts and concerns. Kulav's mother was in dire condition. Every day that passed saw her worsen in her catatonic state. The kingdom was far from fully in the God-King's grasp, as threats from within and without endangered all he held.

Though from out of the darkness, her lover, her King, arose.

Dark as night itself, with ebon hair that seemed to be blacker still, Kulav was immense. A mountain of a man that surpassed the size of even most of his savage kin out of the north. He was glorious, she thought, the glint of moonlight upon his dark muscles, outlining the ridges of his bulging sinew.

From the moment she had laid eyes upon him, she was filled with awe and a sense of knowing. Intuitive knowledge that he was no mere mortal man, but a God-King upon the earth.

No matter how time changed her—from a lowly servant to the Queen at his side—she still felt it when she looked at him. Felt it in her heart, and in her loins.

"You are troubled," he said, his deep, dark voice so husky and booming. Even as he spoke delicately in the middle of the night, his powerful words resonated through the room, out of the canopy bed.

That big, strong hand of his reached out, its hardened touch stroking over her belly, feeling her pale flesh and the swollen life within. His touch, though, was like no ordinary man's. His touch made her skin electric and did things to her even in the fullness of pregnancy that made her want to be so utterly, utterly bad for him.

All it took was sight of him. The touch was only fuel to the flames.

As she watched him in the pale moonlight, her eyes slipped down, drinking in his glorious nudity. The most stunning male form she could have ever gazed upon. Down over stony abs that were as hard as the mountain Ariste itself to the thick, engorged length of her King's ever needful cock.

Without a single conscious thought, her knees raised and parted. She was worse than a bitch in heat for him, and her moistening cunny wept for want of his presence inside of her.

"Just a bad dream," she said, her soft voice so much less sultry than her old one, though it was slowly warming to her. It took time getting used to a body not her own.

"Nothing to trouble a God-King," she added on with an adoring smile.

Mirella had everything she'd yearned for. She'd married the God-King, she was swollen with his child once more. Yet at such a cost.

"You have had so many of those as of late," he said, leaning in and kissing her shoulder. His moist lips trailing down, just as his fingers rounded her belly and edged towards her bare cunny in like fashion. "What drives them, my love?"

Nothing could do justice to what it meant to hear those deep, gravelly words from the lusty voice of the God-King himself. Each husky syllable a quiver down her spine that dampened her loins further, so that as his fingers trailed along her bare slit, he found a slick reservoir of her desire.

"It's nothing, your Greatness," she said, her own breathing having grown heavier, almost panting. She struggled to even remember what troubled her any longer, for a switch had been flipped the moment she laid eyes upon him in the dark. Her dainty, pale hand already reaching to his manhood, touching upon that ebon pillar with such reverence. Such worship.

It had given her two children already, and doubtless many more to come. And more than that, it had given her all of the most satisfying sexual experiences of her life.

Had stolen her second-life's virginity from her on their wedding night.

His full lips kissed upon her engorged breast, and for a brief moment she found herself once more lamenting that they were not as large as they were when she lived in the body of Mirella. Though Kulav showed no disappointment, lusted for her still, that only eased her mind a little.

Gone was the olive skin, in its place was a fairer peach. Her supple curves shrunk into dainty proportions, her dark hair turned golden.

She wondered if there'd ever be a time when she could look in the mirror and not expect to see someone else staring back at her.

"I can have the Royal Apothecary make something for you to help you sleep soundly, my love," he husked in between smacks of his lips, sliding his tongue out to lash at her areola as he tugged the gauzy nightdress down, exposing her stiffened teats.

How times could change.

It was only a couple years before that she was a cowering servant, watching her city burn, her owners crumble and die. Then, as things were at their bleakest, she saw him: the ebon god who kissed and suckled at her teat, who had given her two children, and so much more. He had made an amazing first impression, to say the least. And that first image of him, towering and terrifying, beautiful yet masculine, had never faded.

Not as she got to know him deeper.

His greedy tongue tugged at her teat as his hand reached over, to expose the other, to sink his dark fingers into her tender flesh and knead it. She had just awoken in a panic, but it never ceased to amaze her how quickly his mere presence managed to pull her from her worries, and into a state of heated lust.

"It's okay, my King," she said in response, her every word so breathy and insatiably reverential. She stroked her fingers over his black glossy hair, as her other hand reached around her pregnant belly, and those dainty digits touched upon his manhood. The dark pillar such a monument to his greatness, and she adored doting upon it.

She had spent countless hours praising at the altar of his masculinity, and learned every inch of that beast of a cock. Though someone came between them then.

"Ah!" the Queen cried in pain, relinquishing his manhood to cradle her belly.

Kulav rose up, needing no more to figure the situation out.

"It's time," he said with a deep certainty to his voice.

"It's time!" she replied with a vehement nod.

"Nursemaids!" came his bellowing cry, and in mere moments, the whole of the palace was in an uproar.

CHAPTER 3

Being called forth to serve as one of the God-King's warrior-concubines was supposed to be a tremendous honour. And it had been, for years. In fact, Yvel's mother was oh so proud of her for being called upon. Her mother still remained up north in the steppes, tending to their people's herds, making sure something of the old ways remained as their newly conquered lands of Ariste brought them wealth and power of another sort.

Dressed in the garb of a warrior-concubine, Yvel had no issue with its skimpiness. The northern tribes often eschewed clothing in the warmth of summer, revelling in the sun and heat after the long winters. Though it was not summer, and wearing little more than boots, belt and cloak felt strange to her. It was unnatural.

Part of her wondered if it wasn't so much the off-season dressing that bothered her as the notion of serving the God-King. Back north she had been left with the responsibility of tending to the herd when her father went to war. She had gotten used to answering to nobody.

That stubbornness, as her mother called it, etched itself in her lovely features, leaving her with a scowl that was all too hard to wipe away.

As dawn approached, she stood watch on the castle ramparts, overlooking not the city below, but the expanse of fields to the north. Out there, somewhere before valleys disappeared into eternal snow and ice, was her mother. Her old life.

Though she was lost in thought too deeply, because an old Crone of the warrior-concubine caste had slipped up beside her. Her hair was silvery-grey, and though she had to be three times Yvel's age, at least, she was fit and hearty. Ka'reem who weren't didn't tend to last long, after all.

"You are a sister with a great burden upon your shoulders, young one," she said to Yvel, her wizened voice steady.

Yvel wished to bite back, but she had learned from her mother well enough to pay respects to elders at least.

"Much indeed, Elder," she said simply, softening her scowl if not bowing her head in deference.

It was just the two of them out there in the early morning, the cool breeze wafting beneath their dark cloaks against their bare skin.

"You are troubled by what's to come for you," the Crone said simply, Yvel's gaze darting in her direction. The elder woman raised her hand in defense. "It is normal. We do not talk of such things, but all are nervous as they await their time to serve the God-King."

Yvel softened, if only a bit.

"Serve him, bear his child, and then be on about your life," the old woman said, offering unasked-for advice. Which made Yvel feel shocked.

"Surely that was not your path, Elder Sister," she said, looking the woman over.

"No, it was not. But times are changing, young one," the old woman cast her gaze back at the castle, some lights dotting the windows. "Our people are penned in here. Our King is adapting. Changing."

Yvel's brow furrowed, but only for a moment.

"I shall do my duty. Return to the north, where my mother shall help raise my child as I tend to the herd," Yvel insisted with certainty.

"That would be wise. In normal times," she said, trailing off.

"What do you mean, Crone?" Yvel responded, brow arched.

"I mean," she said, sliding in closer to the younger woman, speaking in quiet tones, "Had you arrived in His service but a couple years ago, you would have promptly found yourself in his bed, pretty as you are. He would have gifted you with child, and your life would be blessed."

She stopped there, even though Yvel waited.

"And now?"

"And now," she said, licking her lips, speaking cautiously, "you shall join the numerous other young woman here - beautiful though they may be - and wait. Just wait."

"Wait for what?" Yvel said, looking bothered by it all. The cool air upon her bare, white skin, the way the metal upon her adornments chilled in the absence of the sun's warmth. She was used to the cold, but for some reason... she felt more exposed than when she was caught on the rocky slopes of the hills in a gale out of the north.

"Wait for *her* to decide he may seed you," the old Crone said, eyes narrowed in distaste.

"Her? Her who?" Yvel said, confused and irritated. She didn't want to wait it out longer than need be. She wanted to fuck the God-King, and get on with her life. She'd never seen the man before, and wasn't struck with the doe-eyed fawning of the other patiently waiting girls, after all.

"The Queen," the Crone said, the word sounding like it was bitterness upon her tongue. "She has snared our King, and now dictates to him when and who he may bed. As if he were some common man."

Yvel stared out, wondering what it all meant for her and her life plans.

"So you may be waiting here a very long time indeed, poor child," the elder woman said, reaching over and patting Yvel's wrist.

Yvel, however, was bothered immensely.

"My mother needs me back with the herd. I can't stay here forever, to serve some trumped up Queen," she said with frustration.

"There is no changing it, young one, but…"

"But? Yes, what is it!"

The old woman shot her a look, but smiled all the same.

"There is something you could do with your time here. Some of us old Crones remember things of long ago. And can help give you the skills you need to return home more than merely a retired concubine-warrior. And maybe with a slice of revenge too."

She looked so smugly proud of herself, but Yvel was intrigued.

"Tell me. If I have so much time to spare, then surely you can show me some of what you mean," she retorted, ever the stubborn one.

"Come," the older woman said, waving her on with her as she began to turn towards the stairs down the ramparts. "I shall show you our little coven. It is due time we invited into our fold some new blood."

CHAPTER 4

Giving birth to Kulav'ar had been trying, immensely so. The son of a God-King had not come into the mortal world easily, Mirella thought. But his second son? By the howling northern wind, it was a miracle she survived it.

"This body was not built for birthing the son of a God, my King," she said, her voice soft and a little listless as her bed was carried along upon a palanquin. The warmth of summer was fast approaching, and Kulav had arranged to have her taken out into the fields beyond the city walls. However, she had been too weary still from the painful, life-threatening childbirth to do anything, even though it was weeks ago. So instead, her, her bed and everything in it, was lifted and carried out of the castle in a regal parade.

It was a show of excess, but one she was grateful for after so long inside.

"Is the fresh air not pleasant, my love?" came her King's deep, husky voice as he sat there upon the side of the bed, overlooking her and the large, dark-skinned child they had made together. Looking upon him it was enough to make one cringe at the thought of him passing through her dainty, delicate body.

"It is indeed," she said, smiling at him, the blue skies and green, grassy fields. Then at their newest child, Malak, who rested in her arms peacefully. "I have been confined to bed for too damn long, my King," she said with a mischievous twist to her pink lips that made the stoic warlord grin.

"You shall recover in due time, my sweet. Do not rush it," he said, reaching out with his long, bare arm from beneath his half-cloak, grasping her leg and squeezing it as he strode along the sides of the covered litter she rode in.

He was beauteous, day or night. Though it seemed that the sun or moon brought out aspects of him that the other could not. He strode in the spring sun, high boots, tight leather pants, and little else but his half-cloak draped over one shoulder. His ebon torso exposed, glistening in the sun unlike the other hairy forms of the Ka'reem men that lifted and carried her carriage.

"I have a meeting with the Imperial representative this evening," he said, and she noted he didn't say 'we', which was a change brought on by her present condition. But it was nothing she wanted to hear, and Kulav used his words sparingly. "I will sort out the issues we have been having as of late with bandits on the southern roads. They have not been patrolling it as they had in the past."

"And why wasn't I invited?" The words slipped out of her mouth before she could even realize what she was saying. Or why she said it. The answer was obvious, and asking the question served no purpose but to antagonize her King.

Though perhaps it was the fact she carried yet another of his children in her arms that he merely gave her a hard look.

"Because you have not been out of bed in weeks. And because it is I, and I alone, that rule," he said, his deep, dark voice steady and even, betraying no anger. He was ever in control of himself, after all.

The Queen bit her tongue, pale cheeks rouged with embarrassment. Why had she done that? Her mind was in turmoil when one of the palanquin carriers erred.

"Watch what you're doing!" she bit at him reflexively, as if haranguing one of the beefy Ka'reem that carried her litter would deflect from her own embarrassment and powerlessness.

Kulav however, furrowed his brows at her then held up a hand, motioning the whole caravan to a stop as he rounded about to the front.

"What is it?" he asked in his firm, commanding voice. For though they were well guarded, with Ka'reem horsemen flanking their processing on all sides, with scouts ranging for miles around to see to their safety, Kulav was not one to take any situation lightly. Especially not where his bride and child were concerned.

"My God-King, something is not right," said the large, hairy man, wearing only a leather harness across his chest.

"How so? Explain," Kulav commanded.

"The ground, it is… it's like—" he cut off, unable to explain himself fully. Though no more words were needed, for Kulav looked about them, his keen eyes needing but a moment for him to determine the situation.

His sabre slid from his lavish scabbard, and he let loose a cry.

"To arms!" he bellowed, the force of his voice like a loud clap of thunder over the steppes, and all around them the whole procession sprang to action. The Queen watched as her King came to life, and the petty outburst was forgotten in less time than it took for her heart to beat.

Never before had she seen Kulav in action in a real confrontation, but there before her she watched as from out of the ground rose the trap prepared for them. Bandits, thugs, assassins, whatever they were, they had hidden beneath the sod and rose up all around and amid their ranks. They brandished mainly daggers and swords and a melee broke out.

Mirella had trained with the warrior-concubines in combat, gotten better at it, but in her condition she could barely walk after narrowly surviving birth. So instead she clutched her child and attempted to shield him as she laid back and watched in shock.

The Ka'reem warriors were the finest fighters in all the known world, and they defended their God-King with a fury unknown elsewhere, but even they could be taken by surprise. Their cries rose, but the silent ambushers went in with short blades glistening in the midday sun.

Blood was splattered upon the ground, but the Queen's eyes were upon her King. As immense as he was, he moved nimbly, when one of the guards was cut down, he stepped in and flourished his blade against the attacker. It was clear Kulav was the far superior fighter, but Mirella cried out in terror as she saw another take advantage of his momentary focus on that fight and raced in for a knife in Kulav's side.

Instead of the God-King falling to that blade, however, he sidestepped, avoided the plunging blade, and then planted his own immense fist into the man's jaw. A loud crack resounded, the assailant went sprawling to the ground, and as the other attacker tried to capitalize upon his target's split attention, Kulav instead lured him in and lopped off his head with a single swipe of his impressive sabre.

It was a glorious display, though it was short lived, because soon Mirella noticed that all around them the chaos was going ill. Most of the guards were kept at a distance, prepared for an assault from all sides but above or below. So while Kulav handled the attackers immediately in his vicinity, his men were not quite as adept.

To her right, the Queen watched as one of the assailants murdered a personal warrior-concubine guard of hers, a woman she had fought with during the early days of the occupation. She had no time to mourn, however, because the murderer was coming for her next.

Kulav guarded her on the other side, but he could not get to her in time, she realized. She inwardly cursed how the strenuous birth had left her lower body strained and weak, though she focussed her will upon the muscle and sinew, willed it to knit tighter and lift her.

From some well deep within, she managed to roll away from the attacker with her baby cradled in arms carefully, to watch as the dagger plunged into the rich silk sheets and mattress.

"Protect your Queen!" bellowed the command from Kulav, who turned to witness the close-call, and the guards rushed to kill the man that had nearly gotten her.

It was madness, and everywhere she looked, Mirella could see crisis or danger. Her legs were working again, and she'd found a reservoir of strength within her somehow, but she was still cradling their child and handicapped by it all. Kulav, however, kept close by as he fought off another assailant.

As soon as one went down, two more came at them. Kulav ripped his velvet half-cloak off and tossed it into the face of one man before slashing open another's chest. Out of his leather pants, he pulled a second long-knife, and Mirella got to appreciate the true depths of her God-King's martial ability, how he had personally cowed the northern tribes of Ka'reem and united them under his brutal rule.

Through the chaos she realized someone had to watch out for other threats, and she focussed her senses like never before. She extended out her focus, looked beyond the immediate area which Kulav had covered, and saw one of the attackers preparing a mini-crossbow.

"Bow!" she cried, pointing at the would-be killer. Though the assassin was too far out to be stopped in time.

Prepared to protect what was his at any cost, Kulav stepped in front of her, and though she stared in abject horror, wishing to stop him, he took the arrow that was clearly intended for her. It plunged right into his shoulder and Kulav grit his teeth.

"Circle the Queen!" he commanded his remaining guards, yanking one in to form a human shield about her. Though even that crossbow bolt in his flesh didn't stop him from charging ahead.

He left her behind the wall of human flesh as he charged at the bowman. The woman who had just stuck an arrow into him was instead fumbling for her short-blade, though she couldn't manage it in time. Kulav cut her down and moved onto the next, even with only one arm able to function fully.

The battle slowly wound to a close from there, the God-King shouted commands and with the Queen offering insight he managed to round up his remaining forces and organize them to crush the assault entirely.

Mirella had no time to wonder how her senses of hearing and sight seemed to so keenly focus in that moment, how her formerly weak and ravaged body managed to pull itself so ably together.

Finishing off their attackers and rounding up a couple survivors, Kulav barked commands at his men before returning to Mirella's side. He wiped the blood from his sword and sheathed his weapon, his dark body spattered with the signs of victory, and his mighty form showing no sign of weakness even as a crossbow bolt stuck out of him.

"You are alright," he said, looking her over, sounding surprised. Somehow she had managed to come out of the fight better than when she began it, after all.

"I'm fine," she said, cradling their child in her arms as she still tried to come to terms with her unscathed survival herself.

The outer guards rode in upon their horses, and Kulav summoned them with a hand gesture. He directed one of the horsemen down and then lifted Mirella up off her feet and onto the beast.

"We must get back to the city as swiftly as caution allows," he instructed.

"I do not believe for one moment that this was anything but an assassination attempt," he added in quiet, for Mirella's ears alone.

"Have the Imperial Commander ready to see me when I get back!" he bellowed at one of the messengers, who spun his horse around and took off at top speed.

The God-King climbed atop her steed, putting his arms around Mirella as he led the way back, but as they rode back towards the city, she couldn't help but wonder at what happened with herself.

Her lower body had felt shredded, useless after the pregnancy. But as the crisis mounted and she found herself laying there, helpless, she willed her limbs to heal. And it was as if they obeyed.

Her legs felt a little tender, like they were new and untouched. But otherwise... she felt fine. Those legs of hers felt stronger and more nimble than ever, even.

She shook it off, however.

Maybe the whole long recovery was in my head, and I just needed time to relax.

CHAPTER 5

The God-King stormed into the palace, heedless of the healers who attempted to treat his wound from the battle. They fussed and scurried to keep up with their towering leader, unable to do much of anything with him in such a fury.

As per his instructions, there awaited the Commander in charge of the Imperial forces still lingering in the city.

He was a tall man for his kind, though nowhere near the staggering height of Kulav. His garb was part studded leather and part colourfully decorated linen, in the style of the southerners. He was bearded with brown hair, with his own appeal, though none of it held a candle to the God-King himself.

"Lieutenant Adom Frenel, Commander of the Imperial expedition to—" the title announcement from the Commander's clarion-holder was interrupted by the God-King.

"Expedition? Do not make me laugh," Kulav said with a sneer as the Queen followed behind, her legs carrying her quickly to keep up with the long strides of her King.

"I have heard of the attack, Your Excellency. A most heinous tragedy," Commander Adom said, his voice low and calm, with a hint of a nasally sound.

Kulav climbed the stairs to his throne, the large, obsidian monstrosity looking like a blight upon the otherwise opulent and exquisite room, its black steel, bones, and raven's feathers such a contrast to the white marble and colourful stonework.

He spun about, looking like a wraith, an instrument of barely suppressed rage with his fists clenched.

"Everyone leave," came Kulav's thunderous command as he sat back upon his immense throne. "Except you," he said, pointing at the Commander.

The whole court scurried to obey, even the officers of the God-King's army. Mirella stayed behind, though, rounding the throne to stand behind his right arm.

In a matter of moments, the great hall was silent, and only three remained. The stiff Commander holding his place, though instead of defiant or uncowed he merely conveyed a prissy sort of imperial stiffness with his stance.

"This assassination attempt was unacceptable!" Kulav roared, slamming his fist down upon the arm of his throne, a fire in his dark eyes as he glared at the man before him. The statement echoed through the halls, and only the great doors to the room kept his words from travelling out to the dismissed masses.

"I was only aware of a bandit attack, your Excellency, a most regrettable by-product of—" but Adom was cut off.

"The lack of Imperial forces guarding your northern reaches," the Queen interjected, pushing herself forward, haughtily. She did not appreciate being pushed aside so easily.

Adom gave a crisp bow to the woman, acknowledging her almost more than Kulav. Though the reasons were clear: the Princess had been an Imperial supporter before her kingdom—and her very body—were taken from her.

"Your Majesty, regrettably, while my forces would normally be tasked with guarding the northern reaches and ensuring its safety, we are tied down here, overseeing the realm and making sure the commoners do not rise up against their new rulers."

"Save the horse shit for the farmer's fields, Frenel," Kulav took control of the conversation again. "We are more than capable of such a thing, and the doors are shut, so the time for indirect talk is over."

The God-King rose back up, towering up over them all once more.

"What happened today was no mere bandit attack. The northern fields are *my* people's domain," he roared, thumping his fist to his chest. "Bandits are no issues there. We take care of them long before they can make it that far!"

Kulav was losing control, and the Queen put her hand upon his bicep, but he ignored it.

"These attackers were no mere bandits! They were professional assassins, able to sneak into *my* realm and lay in wait for us. They knew our very route!"

Such a furious figure, Mirella had trouble not being distracted by him. His broad shoulders back, his bloodied torso heaving with anger, showing off the many peaks and troughs of his sculpted, manly physique.

Her earlier, wounded ego had already faded into nothingness.

He looked like a champion gladiator in the middle of a bout in the coliseum rather than a King.

"This was an Imperial operation! An attempt to have me and my lineage killed!" he said, his heavy, booted feet moving down the steps of the dais.

"Your Excellency…" Adom sputtered, his prissy countenance wavering. "If such is true, I have no knowledge of it, and as First Cou—"

Kulav drew his obsidian dagger from his leather legguards, the dark metal gleaming in the lights of the hall, his eyes full of rage and murder.

"Do you even know why we discuss this in private, fool?" came the God-King's guttural, growling words, so low and gravelly as they rumbled out of his barrel chest.

"To come to some agre—" Adom attempted to answer, but Kulav put the words into his mouth as Mirella watched on, inarguably titillated by the display of her King and Husband asserting himself upon the lesser lord.

"Because if I had uttered one word of suspicion about your and your people's actions before my men, you would already be dead and war would be upon us. You, most simple of fools, have overstepped your bounds."

Adom backed away as Kulav slowly approached with dagger brandished steadily in his hands.

"Your temporary garrison would be massacred, but my new subjects in the streets would suffer for the combat. And after their long, arduous adaptation to my rule, I do not wish them to hurt needlessly any longer."

"I understand, Your Maj—" Adom was cut off again as Kulav closed the gap and the Commander's back was put to the marble pillar. The tip of the dagger raised up, pricking beneath his jaw.

"Your expedition rushes home now. My patience is at an end. You have until sundown to be gone from the city walls and to be making your way home across the fields, in double-time. My forces shall escort them along the way, and ensure you do not deviate from these directions in the slightest."

Kulav's dark eyes were fiery, lit red with rage as they flared wide.

"Do you hear me?" he growled, and Adom nodded.

"Good," was the God-King's response, slow to pull the dagger away and point it at the door.

"Now go!"

With that, Kulav was done with the simpering man, and even the Commander knew better than to offer another objection. He scurried across the marble, even slipped in his hurry, barely catching himself in time.

Though once he was gone, the enraged God-King didn't fully deflate.

Instead, he slipped his dagger back into his sheathe and turned around to face his Queen.

"Are you sure that was wise, my King?" Mirella said, for though she was flustered by the display, some part of her prodded her to be troublesome. To say things she knew better than to say in a moment like that.

Kulav climbed the steps in silence towards her.

"The Empire can boast of a military that outnumbers ours twenty to one, perhaps forty to one," she said calmly.

Though her calm was dispelled once he was upon her, his powerful arms grabbing her.

"You push me too far, my pet," he growled at her, and after only the briefest of pauses he lunged.

And their lips pressed together for a hard, passionate kiss.

The Queen was so dainty and diminutive, pale and pristine in appearance. She was the polar opposite of her King, who was huge, dark and bloodied from his battle.

Yet when they came together like that, they formed a beautiful union. Her gossamer gown pressed against his dirty leather, and his powerful arms crushing her against his body.

The fires that burned within him were not easily extinguished, Mirella knew that. She had been the vessel of his doused tempers many a time, after all. Or more accurately, the lucky recipient of his enflamed lusts.

Those two big, strong hands of his groped at her body, feeling her dainty frame, her perky rear, and they lifted her up off the marble floor with such ease. The smacking of their lips resounding in between the flicks of his tongue and the bites of his teeth upon her pouty lower lip.

Mirella had feared at first that the God-King would not like her new form, that he'd find her displeasing with how dainty and youthful she was. And another part of her had been afraid that perhaps he'd like her better, that he'd find her more appealing than the form she was given at birth.

It was complicated, and yet when finally his hands and mouth pressed against her, those concerns died down, replaced with the lust she'd always had for him.

Ever since she first saw him, her need and desire for him hadn't dimmed, and in the wake of his anger, no less so.

Her gossamer dress was pulled up over her silky skin, the translucent fibers revealing her svelte form and clinging to the slight curves that childbirth had granted her.

The neck of her gown rose up her to her jaw, but the God-King grasped a hold of that fine material and tore it, exposing her soft, ivory skin beneath. Those ravenously hungry lips of his kissing and suckling at her tender flesh as he held her in his grasp.

"You incite my passions too dangerously, pet," he growled at her, nipping her smooth skin between his teeth as he squeezed her frame in his strong, groping grasp.

The vessel that Mirella inhabited was soft, its nerves not used to harsh touches even after the intervening months, and it made her squeak a little, but her lust hadn't changed. Mentally, she craved it, his cruel, teasing kisses and nips, the way he manhandled her and lost himself to her body.

"My King," she cooed, grinding in against him, her hand seeking that stiffening pillar beneath his leathers, "I've missed your touch."

That elicited a low growl from the giant of a man, and he squeezed her pert rear as her delicate fingers traced the outline of his thick, throbbing cock.

That massive pillar of flesh strained his leathers in such a lewd display, hiding little from the imagination. She deftly undid the straps and buckles, and the garment sprang free from the pressure of containing so much meaty cock.

At last her hand found that pulsating girth, the veins along it so rigid and full, and her every soft touch upon it made him groan and growl further.

Kulav lowered her down to the marble floor, atop the dais, crouching down along the stairs as he continued to kiss her flesh and pull her dress open further, his need to expose her to his hungry lusts insatiable.

She'd been incapacitated for what had felt like so long, and the desperate touches of her lover brought her to a higher point of arousal than she could remember.

It was the simple, undeniable truth, and as he exposed her glistening sex to the air, there was no hiding it.

She stroked him, feeling out his throbbing veins, remembering each little valley and curve with such fondness. It was larger than she could recall, though, and it looked obscene in that dainty hand of hers.

Those ivory digits contrasted so starkly to the obsidian of his manhood. Yet it was strikingly beautiful all the same, how much they looked unalike. Their spawn - both past and future - destined to be a melding of a dark God and a beautiful fairy of a woman.

Kulav took hold of her legs, spread them back with her heels still upon her feet. He splayed her open so wide upon the royal dais, and had anyone been there to watch it would have been an obscene sight to make of royalty.

Though Kulav cared not, and kissed from her ankle on up to her knee, tasting her smooth, pale flesh. The luscious, hungry kisses landed upon her flesh as his dick pulsated before him, so thick and needy for her.

She was a slave to his desires, and moaned as her back arched towards him. For all the things Mirella had lost in the transfer of her body for the then-Princess's, flexibility and agility were gained. She couldn't handle the brutal blows so well, but she was better able to contort to fit his brutish form.

Her skin tickled with his kisses, with his hungry mouth devouring her creamy flesh. She'd been untouched for too long, and it gave her a higher sensitivity.

Not that such things were ever needed when your lover was a God amongst men. His every kiss, his every touch was like the ignition of a flame.

He moved on down her soft inner thigh, smacking his lips against her flesh as he moved towards her slick cunny. Her pink petals of hers glistened, too long unfulfilled.

Kulav stared at them for but a moment, before his own hungry need overtook him and he lunged for her. He ate her pussy, absolutely devoured it with his hunger for her flesh.

It was a lewd sight, with the moist sounds of her slit upon his mouth smacking, then the work of his tongue began. The swirls about her sensitive clit, the lashes and prodding. He was insatiable.

And Mirella knew, in that moment, how truly blessed she was.

To have him lust for her, to have him return to her time after time - despite the taboo of him taking a woman while she was pregnant - was a wonderful burden for her to bear.

Her body jerked and spasmed, the sensations flooding her and making her every nerve light up with excitement. She glanced down, looking at him between her splayed thighs and it was one of the most enticing things she could've imagined.

"Yes!" she cried out, her hips thrusting towards him.

She knew of course, that he did it for his own pleasure. His excitement for her flesh drove him to experience her in every which way.

Nonetheless, the thrill of having such a man as him, the God-King himself, eating her out, bringing her such pleasure… it had a way of making her feel dizzyingly powerful. Even as his strong hands gripped her thighs, holding them in place so tight to keep her in his preferred positions.

The God-King continued to lash his tongue over her slit, around her clit, prodding that sensitive bud until she could no longer take it. She began to flail and struggle, but it was all in futility, because he held the reins of power, and kept her in position as he ate his fill.

There was no use fighting against him, but still she instinctively struggled in vain, trying to escape that encompassing bliss that was quickly overwhelming her. Words and thoughts all evaporated into the background, leaving in their remains the thrill and excitement of the moment.

"Yes!" she cried out, her body toppling quickly towards the edge, until she was nothing more than a spasming mess, fueled only by her electric orgasm.

Vision betrayed her then, sight becoming nothing more than dizzying lights as her senses were overwhelmed with such an earth shattering climax. Made all the more intense by the fact the God-King refused to let up, provoking her sensitive flesh throughout the whole intense orgasm.

She became so lost in it all, she barely even registered that he pulled away, licked his lips and - while still holding her legs in place - slid the engorged tip of his manhood along her glistening, wet slit.

That touch was what brought her back to awareness however, the feel of her petals being forced to flower about the broad, dark-purple crown of his manhood. Slowly, slowly it sank in, stretching her cunny once more, readjusting her to the limits of his girth.

It brought with it her senses, his cock calling her back to reality, forcing her to feel his maleness as he splayed her around it. She glanced down, watching in awe as he split her open, that dark shaft disappearing into her wettened, pink slit.

She let out a desirous groan before her head tilted back, her eyes fluttering shut.

Kulav draped her slender legs over his broad shoulders and bent over her body.

His intense dark eyes bored into her, watching as he began to loosen her up with short, shallow thrusts of his hips, that thick tool of his gradually widening her slick little cunny, stretching her back to accommodate his length.

He growled and grunted, looking at her with such intense desire as his heavy balls swung beneath him, smacking against her pale ass.

He was as entranced by her as she was with him, watching her smaller body bounce upon his cock as he plowed into her.

Though his ravenous hunger for her flesh caused him to reach up, grasp her dress and yank it down, exposing her chest to his groping hand. Her tits pressed into his palm as he squeezed and kneaded the flesh, watching her pink nipple poke between his thumb and index finger.

It stiffened readily against his hard touches, and she arched into it, craving his brutality. The way he made her feel so alive, igniting her fire like she'd never believed possible before meeting him.

Her body was still affected with the tremors of her climax, and each thrust brought another jolt of pleasure through her.

The God-King took her upon the pristine marble floor of the throne room, countless generations of Aristean monarchs - men and women who owned people like they owned cattle, who commanded armies - and sullied it with their carnal act of passion and lust.

Mirella tried to hold onto the floor for support, but the marble was smooth and all there was that kept her from slipping away was her lover's strong grasp. The way he held her hip and breast, kept her pinned beneath him as he pistoned his dark shaft into her faster, harder.

"You're mine, pet. Forever mine. Say it!" He commanded with a harsh, gravelly voice.

It was an easy thing to admit to, for she felt it, deep within her soul. From the first moment she laid eyes upon the conqueror, she knew that there was always going to be a piece of her heart, her body, for him and him alone.

The words, though, did not come so easy. Through pants, and gasping, she struggled to make them form upon her lips.

"I'm yours," she finally managed, her usually dulcet voice turned husky with her desperate moans.

She was rewarded for her obedience with his rough squeeze of her chest and a frenzied stab of his cock into her depths. Rough and hard, he thrust into her again and again, jarring her whole body, filling her to capacity and seemingly beyond with how his dick swelled and throbbed.

Her little cunny turned into a sleeve for his cock, barely able to contain him.

"I'm going to cum," he growled out, panting and grunting.

That big, broad, bare chest of his, bulging with muscle, glistening with a thin sheen of perspiration that highlighted every mound of finely honed sinew.

Perhaps she should be concerned, given the ferocity of her last pregnancy, but instead she reveled in bringing him to that brink of pleasure. She was greedy for him, possessive, and her fingers dug into his back, holding him to her as be began to tremble.

Just moments before he found his peak, however, he reached down from her waist, rubbed his thumb over her clit and brought her quaking into new bliss.

"Cum on my cock," he growled in command as he bucked his hips and grunted, his dick swelling, his motions becoming erratic.

He was a beast of a man, all those gorgeously powerful muscles put towards fucking her and then… he came. He blew his load like a thick torrent, that rich, milky cream filling her depths and flooding her fertile depths so soon after she had given birth to his last child, crying out in wild pleasure.

Her arms wrapped around him, her own mind hazy as she jerked and spasmed around his member, her entire body responding with such ferocity to his pleasure. To bring him to the peak had always been one of her greatest joys in life.

Together they slowly climbed down from their peak, the God-King's thick arms slowly wrapping about her as he leaned in and kissed her upon the lips. Her own cunt's tang was still rich upon his mouth as he pressed such a passionate kiss to her, his dick still pulsating as the last spurts of his seed deposited inside her.

Though as much as part of her wanted it, another part shied from the idea of so soon again becoming pregnant with another of the God-King's children. The taxing toll it put upon her body to carry the child of no mortal man...

Her mind could not linger there long, however, because a woman's voice interrupted them.

"Your Majesty... I come bearing grave news."

CHAPTER 6

Kulav asked for news of his mother's condition every day, but the answer was always the same.

No change.

But that day was different. To have one of the caregivers burst in with news like that was outrageous. Mirella hoped with all her heart that it was just an exaggerated reaction after so long without anything to report.

"Perhaps she's awoken with a new prediction about your course of action," the Queen said, hopeful that's all it was. Though part of her… some small, tiny voice in her head, wanted her to be wrong.

She was still sore after the intense tryst in the throne room, but in yet another emergency, she willed her body to action and it obeyed.

It was a pleasant change for her. Since taking over the Princess's body she had to come to terms with the fact the delicate young woman was weaker and more fragile than she could ever recall being.

The first few months were arduous. For while she felt as strongly as ever for her King and husband, her delicate form could not handle his intense lusts like her old body had been able to. A soft life had not helped the Princess adapt to such vigorous activities.

Those thoughts ran through her mind, and Mirella realized they were in large part distraction, trying to push away the worries and concerns that plagued her as she raced down after her King as he outpaced her.

She arrived in time to see the unthinkable.

The God-King fell to his knees by his mother's bedside, looking crushed.

Mirella rushed up behind him, placing her dainty hand upon the massive man's shoulder and looked on in horror as the pale, spindly frame of his mother - so easily defined through the silks and fabrics of her blankets draped over her - lay still.

Motionless.

Not even the faintest sign of breathing.

"Her breathing is so shallow, I predict she has already begun to pass into the Great White Sky," said the head healer, a woman of great age, with frazzled white hair. She had been attending to the mother of a god for so long, that few other things concerned her.

"How much longer?" Mirella asked as her husband stared upon the woman who gave birth to him, sorrow in his heart if not in his stony face. That much she knew.

"Not long. Minutes, hours. Maybe days, but as I said… she is already gone to us in every way that matters, your Majesties." The healer bowed her head, standing with the other caregivers as they stood by, helpless.

Not even the power of the God-King could undo what was happening.

Silence reigned, but from behind Mirella heard one of the Guard Captains shift anxiously, awaiting orders, of course.

It took a while, but at last Kulav said:

"Escort the imperial forces out of the city. They are making their way home. See that you give them all an honourable death. Show them how it's truly done. Then, no one bother me any further."

It was his final command before he reached out, took his mother's hand.

Mirella watched, winced at how the once-fiery woman had deteriorated, her fingers having withered to little more than bones with pale, translucent skin upon them, all the more stark in contrast to her son's strong, dark flesh.

After the officer left, silence took over once more, and Mirella stood by her husband's side.

Nobody moved, even their breathing seemed to have all quieted to a level that was imperceptible.

None there had gone untouched by the God-King's Mother. Her actions, her sacrifices, had made so much possible. She had not only given birth to a man of great stature and deed, but helped make him a king.

She had sacrificed her body to give birth to him, to see him raised to a man.

She had sacrificed her mind to give him the title he deserved.

Finally, she gave her life to hold onto all that he had accomplished.

Mirella wasn't sure when she fell to her knees, but there she was, clutching the God-King's shoulder as she reached out, took hold of the dying woman's hand same as him.

It was her who helped bring them together, set the pieces in motion, then nudged it all along the way to make sure it occurred. She felt a bond with the woman, and not only because they both loved the man that was Kulav, and the God-King he'd become.

She had bestowed upon Mirella knowledge of powers and things that absolutely destroyed her perception of reality. Had given her a new life, quite literally.

So when she saw the woman's lips move after touching her, her eyes welled with tears of joy. But when she blinked away the moisture, she saw the woman hadn't moved at all, and Kulav, who was staring intensely, showed no signs of having seen a thing.

It confused her, but then she felt a squeeze of her hand, and when she looked down saw that nobody had moved. That the dying woman's hand still lay limp, Kulav's still focussed upon his mother's last touch.

You have changed, came a wispy, quiet voice seemingly from out of nowhere.

And must change again, it continued.

Ours is sacrifice, and yours are far from over.

Mirella felt a chill up her spine, knowing somehow - innately, magically, she couldn't say - that she was hearing the witch's dying words in her mind.

You and I can only sacrifice what is ours to give, Mirella... take care of my son.

With that, it all came to an end.

Little changed visibly, but Mirella knew. And so did Kulav.

They had knelt by the dying woman's side for hours by that point, but suddenly... it was as if the air had changed, and everyone caught on one by one after the two closest to her.

The God-King's head sank, his hand slipping from his mother's deceased fingers. He knew.

He had no magic, no sorcery. That much Mirella knew for certain. Neither he nor any of the men of the Ka'reem tribes possessed any magic. It was the lot of womankind.

No, whatever let him know, was something subtler. More personal. A mother-son bond that transcended matters of matter versus magic.

The healers shuffled away in silence, heads bowed. Their duty was done, and the place of the dead would only taint their ability to heal the living it was said. As they left, Mirella knew they would be replaced.

The gentle wails of the mourners came. They were women and men of slight frame, the sickly of the tribes, who survived childhood only through great hardship and miracle, but who had few other abilities to aid the group.

They wore gossamer gowns, all of them, the pale fabric hiding little as they sang their dirge, as per Ka'reem custom.

Kulav and Mirella were unbothered by it, though. Their presence was like a gentle breeze, as they came to perform final rites for the deceased vessel and wish the spirit of the dead a peaceful end that was undisturbed.

Though while they carried out their duties, Mirella did hers.

She looked to the God-King, and though his face was still stony, unmoving, moisture ran down his cheek. For even a god amongst men could be brought to quiet tears in his greatest sorrow.

Mirella wrapped her slender arms about him as best she could and comforted him in continued silence.

CHAPTER 7

Yvel was not privy to the inner secrets of the palace, certainly not after having spent so much time cloistered away with the coven of old crones studying their ways and learning their methods.

In a way, that time had lessened her influence and abilities. But in another, it had granted her insight into how things worked. Given her a purpose beyond waiting for the God-King's blessing.

Yet despite that all, even she heard rumblings of the assassination attempt.

So when the Imperial representative Adom Frenel hurried on by her, she took advantage.

"Leaving our fair city so soon, southerner?" she said.

Her voice was husky and contemptuous to his imperial ears, matching her tall, powerfully framed body. She was a Ka'reem woman through and through, all the more so to his foreign eyes.

Nonetheless, he stopped.

"Yes, urgent matters draw us away. And it's clear we are no longer needed here," he said with a cordial smile, ever courteous. Even when he was playing the viper.

"Your escort awaits you," she said, pointing down in the dim, waning light of the day towards the cavalry that was so emblematic of her people, waiting to guide his troops out.

"Yes, so if you'll excuse me, madam, I must be off," he said with a crisp bow.

But before he could finish the motion, she interjected. "I would not be so hasty if I were you," she remarked, turning towards him with her smug little half-smile.

"I am sorry madam, but we have little choice, time is of the essence," he insisted, anxious to go.

"If you leave now, you will not survive the journey," she said, the words sounding rather profound to his ears.

Though the northern women were said to be mystics and seers, he'd not encountered anything explicitly indicating as such since he'd been sent on the posting.

It had his attention, all the same.

"What do you know?" he asked, clasping his hands behind his back as he walked closer to her.

She was a warrior-concubine, one of a rank he had never encountered before, off limits from contact with men such as him. Though she dared flout the rules. But he was on his way out anyhow.

"Little," she confessed, lifting a brow and peering back out at his own troops, who were hurriedly extricating what they could get of their equipment and loading it aboard wagons and carts. "But I heard tell of an attempt upon the King's life. And now you scurry off. There is only one conclusion to draw."

The man's lips went into a dour, straight line.

"A false accusation, I assure you. Mere coincidence," he said, backing away again, preparing to leave.

"If you understood my people at all, sir, you would be aware that only one fate awaits you outside our gates."

Her dark brown eyes turned back upon him, a grim note to her voice.

He laughed, softly, but laughed nonetheless.

"The Empire is not your people's enemy at present. The King would not risk making us one, I am certain," he rebutted.

"You do not understand. Your people are our enemy. This lull is but time for the God-King to prepare. This attempt on his life merely forces his hand early at worst."

"But why? A diplomatic solution still exists," he insisted.

"Because," she stated imperiously, as if losing patience with is ignorance, "the Ka'reem do not tolerate a weak leader. The God-King is our ruler because he is strong and tolerates no attempt to undermine him. If he let this slight go unaddressed, the tribes would turn against him, or simply start a war without him in his honour. Either way, the result is the same. Except without him taking charge, the war would be unfocused, chaotic."

The Commander's eyes narrowed both in suspicion and deep thought.

"And what choice do I have? Our forces could not win here if we stay. We would eventually be worn down before reinforcements could arrive. It is death either way."

She wore so little even by Imperial standards. A black cloak draped over her shoulders, leather harness that hid little of her pale, fit body. High boots that clung to her calves and knees.

She would look the part of some pleasure dungeon mistress back in the Imperial capital, he thought.

"You could stay. While your men go to be lambs for the slaughter in your place," she said, pursing her lips in some dry amusement.

"And the God-King won't just execute me at his pleasure then?" he said, bothered by the thought.

"Perhaps," she responded with a shrug of her shoulders that made her heavy bosom heave. "But you are a man of thought, are you not? Can you not figure out a solution to your dilemma through bandying words?"

That made him pause and consider.

Though the long silence came to an end when he asked his next question.

"Why do you tell me these things? Why would you want to help me?"

She stepped closer to him, sliding her tongue around her full lips, and though it might've looked sensual on most women, it was almost predatory on her.

"Because," she said, her voice low and soft, "we Ka'reem only follow strong leaders. And some of us believe our King has already been usurped from beneath our noses."

"By whom?" he asked, brow furrowed.

"By the Queen," she replied easily. The two of them were almost the same height, the southern Commander finding himself an inch or so beneath her.

"Helping me could only help her though," he said, not understanding the woman's motivations.

"So be it. Then we have a strong ruler, unencumbered by a weak man," she said haughtily.

Adom pondered her words a while longer.

"If I survive this…" he began.

"Then you owe me," she said, a feral grin on her pale, lovely face.

He felt both excited and bothered by that revelation.

"I must go now if I'm to appoint one of my men to lead," he said.

"Go quickly. But go wisely. And," she said, stopping him one last time as he turned to go, "come and find me if you survive."

"How?" he asked, brow furrowed yet again.

"You'll figure it out."

CHAPTER 8

It was hard to believe preparations could be made for so magnificent a funeral in so little time, but the Ka'reem and citizens of Ariste knew the importance of the occasion. The mother of their God and King was already legend, even when she still lived.

Though part of the Queen winced at the memory it evoked, watching from atop the high perch of the palace, overlooking the city, all the torches and bonfires lit atop roofs and walls was reminiscent of the day the God-King claimed the city for himself.

Mirella didn't understand the emotion that overtook her.

The day Kulav came and laid claim to her was, ironically, the day of her emancipation.

It was the last time she ever felt unappreciated. The last time she felt powerless.

For as much as she served her husband and King, was his heart and soul, she did so willingly. She gave herself to him, and he had not disappointed.

The difference between freedom taken and freedom given with a heartfelt smile was a world apart.

A great dais was carried by throngs of Ka'reem men, and atop it sat a strange bronze dish, the size of a swimming pool, rimmed with raven's feathers. Within it burned a great fire that consumed the lifeless body of the Seer, Kulav's mother.

It was a slow, plodding procession. On down the winding streets of Ariste, past each doorstep, where citizens stood, candles lit in hand as they watched.

Nobody spoke. Not a single word, nor even a cough.

It was silence but for footsteps and the crackle of flame.

Some cried, but those who did sobbed in quiet.

The God-King himself took the lead, despite the recent attempt on his life. His half-cloak hid the wound in his shoulder, and he presented nothing but the image of strength and authority, even as his face was locked in stern sadness.

Much of the night was taken up in the event, because it did not end even when they left the city's gates.

Onward they marched, into the fields, out farther and farther. Not so far as the prior day's assassination attempt, but they came out into the open plains before letting the dais rest.

People cleared from the front of the great bronze funeral pyre, and Kulav ascended the steps alone.

Mirella stood back and watched, candle in hand, as did everyone else who wasn't bearing the load. They observed as their God-King stared into the flickers of flame through the darkness of night.

Still nobody spoke, not for the long hours until, at last, it was done.

The flames died, and all that was left was ash and cinders. It was then that the God-King crouched, his broad body stretching out as he took hold of that massive metal construct. It was hot still, and the scent of burning flesh could be smelled, yet it didn't stop the man.

Mirella winced just watching, knowing the wound in Kulav's shoulder must have made it all an excruciating practice. But there he was, his muscles bulging, biceps so pronounced in the light of moon and flame, as he lifted and tilted the bronze vessel over.

The winds out of the north had been oddly still during their procession, so much so that the Queen worried the funeral rites might not actually work. In fact, she had cursed fortune that they were given the first calm evening in ages on so momentous a moment.

But it seemed no sooner than the flames died that the wind picked up once more.

It was as if the cold, biting northern gale quieted in respect, and came galloping back like the Ka'reem hordes at the beck of their God and His mother.

The contents of the bronze vessel spilled forth, and the icy winds carried the Seer's ashes upon their biting fringes, off towards the south. To Ariste, and beyond.

The silence among them ended at last, as Kulav looked on as what was left of his mother's earthly vessel drifted away. His voice was sombre, but loud.

"Where go her earthly remains to wander, so too shall we. All in due time, Mother."

Only the Ka'reem had followed the procession out into the steppes, and they knew the significance of their King's words. It was more than a son's heartfelt pledge to his departed mother. It was a promise of further conquest to the south.

And in a display that would be considered outlandishly disrespectful most anywhere else, the assembled thumped their left feet in time, building up a tempo that quaked the earth beneath Mirella's feet. Again and again their stomping grew together, louder and louder until the gaps between thuds was filled with a loud, guttural yell from deep within their diaphragm.

They continued like that, looking up at their stoic God-King, on and on it went until Mirella's throat grew hoarse from trying to keep up with the Ka'reem.

Then, from out of the west, it came.

A flaming arrow pierced the sky, then burst into a fiery display.

It was no firework, it did not come from the city. It was a signal.

The colour and display of the burst marked it as a very particular kind of signal, one which all those gathered knew well.

Victory.

The Ka'reem "escort" that had accompanied the Imperial forces out of the city had made use of the night, when other military forces feared to battle. Their prey were all dead, and their God-King had both his personal revenge for the attempt on his and his wife's life and a blood offering in the name of his mother.

Such a thing was not required by tradition. In fact, only the greatest of warlords amongst the Ka'reem's past were known to have had such a thing. Two men down throughout history.

But for the mother of the God-King, for Kulav's mother, a new exception was made.

The pounding and yelling became overlaid with chanting, and then, over top of it all, let cry the God-King's bestial roar.

It was a sound that would be said to echo over the mountains themselves and into the empire beyond. Tales would later tell of an avalanche that night which crushed an Imperial village on the opposing slopes of the mountain.

It was singularly the most significant sound a single man would ever make in all of history, and yet...

For Mirella, watching, it was all about the sadness in the man she loved.

Kulav stood alone, as per tradition.

He stood alone, because his mother now did not even have that.

A reminder, that in the end, all stood alone, and to die was the one burden that the tribe could not help someone bear.

They could only help the living.

CHAPTER 9

The last thing Mirella wanted to do was to leave the God-King's side in the days following the loss of his mother.

But more than her desire to be at his side was the need to take over some of his mundane duties in the period of his mourning. So when the request for a meeting came from the leaders of her fellow warrior-concubines, she thought it was the perfect task to take upon herself so the God-King need not trouble himself.

Though part of her thrilled, was excited to take charge and wanted nothing more.

So she bustled in through the door of the meeting chamber, a former chapel, her long gown flowing behind her. These were women who - all but the newer ones - knew her true identity. Know that she was the "traitor" Mirella in the Princess's body.

But all the same, even one person extra who did not already know that secret was one too many to find out. So the pretense had to be kept up anyhow, sadly.

Though what she wasn't expecting was the surprised look upon their faces as she entered in.

They still rose and paid her the respects they would otherwise, saluting as she took a seat.

Mirella no longer had the body and presence she once did, gone was her attire like the women before her, of raven's feathers and barely-covering clothes. Instead she wore gossamer gowns, woven by the finest tailors of Ariste, flowing behind her.

They weren't altogether staid however. Their fabric was often see-through, showing off the Queen's porcelain skin and dainty figure.

She worked with the metropolitan tailors of Ariste to find a style that blended the old monarchical fashions with that of the new conquerors. Covering yet revealing at the same time.

"Sit, my sisters," she said with a smile as she took her own seat, the others following suit after their Queen.

Silence reigned for a moment before one of the women spoke up.

"Accept our apologies please, Your Majesty, but we were expecting the God-King himself."

"What they mean, Your Majesty, is that they wish to discuss matters of the God-King's breeding," came a familiar voice from the sidelines.

There stood Svella, Mirella's oldest friend amongst the Ka'reem, and comrade during the early days of occupation when they were tasked with retaining control of the city while the God-King was away.

"Svella!" the Queen cried out, rising up from her seat immediately, palms to the table, eyes wide; a great big smile upon her face. "You're back!"

The two women grinned and embraced, although Svella was all the more disproportionately large compared to Mirella in her new body; the tall Amazonian the epitome of what it meant to be a Ka'reem woman.

"I did not expect you to return from your recent birthing so soon, sister!" Mirella said, their embrace ending as they parted and the Queen looked her over. "You are already firm and taut, back in shape," she tacked on, giving the woman's pronounced abs a playful poke.

Svella laughed, holding her raven-plume helm beneath her arm and cloak as she stood before her Queen's inspection.

"You know me, my Queen. I did my duty for my son, and hurried on back to my calling," she declared warmly, no sorrow at having come back to her post so soon.

"Another son," Mirella said with a sigh and a shake of her head. "He is in good hands with your partner."

"Indeed. She lives for the love of family," Svella said proudly.

Though their reunion was interrupted once more.

"Sorry to bother, Your Majesty, but the matter of the God-King's duties remains…" said one of the middle aged women, around Mirella's true age, though a good decade older than her new form.

The Queen tried not to show her distaste for the interruption, but smiled at her friend, guided her to a seat at her side before daintily resuming her own place.

"And what is the matter there, precisely?" she asked, her voice crisp and regal; sounding entirely like Annabelle as she knit her fingers together upon the black marble table.

The women cast furtive glances between one another as Svella and Mirella sat stoic and composed.

"He has not been visiting with the young warrior-concubines," said one of the new sisters, sheepishly.

"His sacred seed has not flowed into the wombs of the new recruits in some time," added in one of the older sisters, using the more flowery language of their order to describe the carnal acts that were part of royal tradition.

Mirella did not miss a beat, however.

"His Greatness is rather absorbed in the mourning of His mother, our dearly departed Seer, and former head of our Order." Her words were delivered crisply and clearly, with all the enunciation that Princess Annabelle's long tutelage provided.

"Of course, Your Majesty. This was not meant to pressure him in his time, we have been seeking an audience since before this all occurred," argued the elder woman who spoke first.

"And unfortunately events have transpired which mean the delaying of the matter, ladies. These things are out of our hands," Mirella said with a faux smile. For some reason she felt defensive, possessive.

In all her time with the God-King, she had accepted that he was no mere man. That she could not have him to herself.

That she could aspire to be his favourite, his confidant, his lover.

But no more.

Somewhere along the lines, a seed of aspiration must have taken root.

"Perhaps, Your Majesty... the devoted young women of his harem could also provide a great deal of relief to His Greatness in His time of need," offered up one of the women, smiling pleasantly.

Mirella's hackles were up at that remark, and in an imperious voice that only the Princess Annabelle could muster, she said:

"You need not worry yourselves. I see to the God-King's relief rather fully. And furthermore, the situation merely provides the women with more time to pursue their training and other duties, while being able to enjoy life in the city."

It was a simple statement to most people, but for the wife of the God-King, it was overstepping. And everyone knew. Even Svella looked at her with arched brow, surprised at the statement.

Mirella rose up from her seat, haughty and regal.

"If that is the only matter to discuss, ladies, then I believe this meeting is adjourned. Thank you for your concerns," she said, giving a plainly false smile as the assembled witches rose up and filed out of the room.

All but Svella at least.

"What? Do you think me wrong, too, sister?" Mirella asked, softening somewhat once it was just the two of them.

"Other than you, I know the God-King better than anyone, Your Majesty." Svella's voice was low, but made softer as she spoke in confidence with Mirella, her friend.

"And?"

"And I know him to be not only in love with you, but madly devoted. Perhaps inappropriately so for a God-King who must rule us all and put his people first and foremost," Svella spoke so smoothly, the words clearly genuine and from the heart.

They made Mirella's resolve wobble, and caused her possessiveness to wane as her eyes watered a little.

"When last he and I were together, I had every sense it would be our last time in service to him like that," Svella said, pausing just a moment. "What you said was undoubtedly correct, and mirrored his own thoughts. However..."

"However?" Mirella asked, looking up at her friend, her own big blue eyes a little misty.

"They were not your words to say, as far as the sisters are concerned. They were the God-King's. And they will react poorly to your having said them in his place."

Mirella felt herself bristle, part of her - some dark little point that didn't wish to be lectured to or told what to do by anyone - didn't care for what she was hearing at all, and wished to admonish Svella for saying it.

Though she knew it to be true, and more than that, valued her friend's words.

"You are right, Svella. I... I got carried away," the Queen said.

"You are under pressure. So much has happened in so short a time, my dear Mirella," she said, reaching out and placing her hand upon the Queen's bare shoulder.

It was a friendly, loving touch, and Mirella welcomed it, even as part of her instinctually said: *a Queen lets no commoner touch her*.

She slumped down into her seat once more in spite of it all.

"I am letting the stress get to me, Svella. That is the only thing I can come up with. This life... was not one I was trained for," she confessed, smiling meekly up at her friend, who smiled back down at her warmly.

"You are bearing the burden well, all things considered. Do not let one stumble let you lose confidence in yourself. The sisters will not turn against you over one misspeak in a private conference."

"Thank you," Mirella said, shutting her eyes a moment and willing calmness through her, forcing back the tears that almost came.

"Now," the Queen said, patting the seat beside her again. "Sit and tell me of your family and your time back home. I have missed you dearly, sister."

Svella sat down as instructed, hunched over, and took the Queen's dainty little hands in hers with a smile.

"With pleasure, Your Majesty. Arga has her hands full with those little brutes..."

Of course, all the while things had been deteriorating faster than either woman realized.

CHAPTER 10

In the halls of the palace outside the conference room, Yvel slunk into a dark corner to meet with one of the old crones of the coven: her co-conspirator.

"The Queen shows her true colours," Yvel said, arching a brow and seeming almost surprised at the flagrant outburst. Such a blatant display of overstepping was clearly not what she had expected. "The Queen has always been so shrewd before now."

"And what do you make of that little development?" the old woman asked, a grin barely visible upon her face as they murmured quietly.

"That she is growing overconfident in her control of the God-King and us," Yvel replies.

"And what shall this mean for us?" the old Crone asked.

"It shall be easier to muster support among the others. They've seen her true colours now, it shall be hard for them to deny the truth when it lies right before them, plain as day," Yvel said, certain of herself as she kept an eye down the corridor, watching for anyone.

"Precisely. Your time shall come, witch. Just wait and see," the old Crone said, a devious glint in her eyes.

CHAPTER 11

Adom wasn't exactly under arrest. He was taken back to his residence in one of the old noble manors that was converted to civic use, though something made the Ambassador doubt it would remain his to use for long.

It wasn't as if it was the most comfortable of places to reside, however. The posh furniture that the former residents owned were looted and claimed by the conquerors, not even as trophies in most cases. Simply looted to fund their new barbaric state.

Instead, the only decorations were those his forces brought with them, with a few cots that once served his soldiers, before he was forced to send all but a few off to their imminent deaths.

The smooth stonework seemed so bleak to his eyes without all the wall hangings and finely crafted furniture. Marble and alabaster bereft of all but the intricate designs that were carved into their very being.

Adom thought that if the hairy brutes were able to easily, they would have taken that as well and sold it.

All sense of security was gone. His remaining guards stood outside, but the God-King's men had stripped them of their weapons and forbade them from carrying any more. He had more secreted away in the manor, though they would do no use anyhow.

How would he survive an actual attempt by the God-King to kill him?

Adom cursed himself, tugging open his Imperial silk cravat and letting his collar hang loose.

"Damnable northern cave," he said, cursing the coolness of the place, and how it never seemed to get as warm as the southern Imperial lands he was so accustomed to.

"Careful, you might offend the mountain itself," came a woman's sly voice.

Adom Frenel looked around before finding the visage of a tall Yvel descending the shadowy stairs off in the corner.

"How did you—" he stopped himself, realizing the question was pointless and dumb.

"I come and go as I please," Yvel boasted, her hair no longer tied back, but let loose. The thick, glossy black strands fanned out around her face, making her face appear all the more lovely.

"Is that to explain why you came and found me instead of vice versa? Because I seem to recall you promising me that I'd need to find you," Adom said, shifting as he studied the woman in her thick, black cloak that covered her whole body, from neck to toes.

"It is all the excuse needed," she said, coming to the bottom of the stairs and resting her hand upon the ornate poster.

"It's not that I'm not pleased to see you," he said, pushing his own fingers through his lengthening dark hair, trying not to act either intimidated or grateful for her presence. He was a trained officer, and appearances could be everything, he was taught.

"Of course not," she said in return, her lips poutily puckered, a saucy sort of expression upon her face that threw him.

"But to what do I owe this visit? After you so graciously gave me the information that saved my life…"

"If only for now," she tacked on.

"If only for now," he agreed.

"Well," she began, twisting toward him and out of the shadows, her hand still upon the railing. Into the light of the room he could see that beneath her cloak she was naked. Or very nearly so.

She had on only some ornate, gemmed brazier and belt, that glittered and drew the eye but did nothing to hide her ample breasts or pink slit.

"I have been given an opportunity. A rare and special one at that," she said, sauntering toward the unsuspecting man, her hips swaying as she slid her hand from the railing and perched it up on her hip, pushing out her cloak to reveal more of her pale, voluptuous figure.

"What sort of opportunity?" was all he could manage to get out, so intimidated and intrigued was he by the northern beauty before him.

His opinions of the brutish, barbaric appearance of all the northerners was also under heavy assault as his gaze trailed down her to stare at her cunny a moment too long.

"The sort that might get me into the God-King's good graces," she remarked, reaching out and touching her fingers to his chest, right beneath his neck.

Those long, slender digits trailed down to his collarbone and nudged his linen shirt open a little wider.

"So then... why are you here?" he asked, distracted by her scent.

Her natural aroma was augmented by something... lavender, he thought? Adding a seductively refined edge to her raw femininity.

"Because I want something from you first," she said, studying his face as his eyes were invariably drawn downwards, to her rather full and perky tits, her nipples showing they at least found his residence a little cool.

"What is that then?" he said, though much of the oomph was gone from his voice. His soft words had little presence behind them.

"I want your guarantee that you will assist me when the time comes that I need it," she said, her voice a little husky, even sultry.

She lifted her other arm, rubbing through his hair, then toying with his ear as she slowly undid the buttons of his shirt.

"What can I possibly provide that you wish now?" he asked, his own breathing growing heavier as his loins responded to the aggressive woman's advances.

"You have some way to get messages through the mountain quickly. Something that the Ka'reem have yet to deduce," she purred.

Her hand had worked open his shirt, and her fingers danced upon his firm stomach before working to loosen his trousers. She took her time, smiling unevenly as she rubbed her digits along the swell of his manhood, tracing it out so brazenly and intimately.

Adom's eyes shut, his pleasure clashing with his best judgment.

"I can't just expose to you any secrets we might have in trade for sex," he said in a murmur as she pressed him up against the big, crude wooden table.

"It's not in trade for the sex we're about to have," she responded.

She squeezed the outline of his shaft through his underpants before tightening her hand in his hair and pushing him down.

"This is just for my amusement and pleasure," she husked.

She lifted one leg up to place her foot upon the table, his face nearly pressed up to her cunt as he went to his knees at her command. The scent of that womanhood strong as he found himself gazing at a glistening slit, already moist with arousal.

"I would be put to death just for this much alone," he said.

Though he had no further time to balk or refuse, because she grasped his dark hair tightly and pulled him into her pussy, his lips and tongue meeting that slick slit as she rocked her hips and ground herself against his face.

"Ohhh," she moaned softly, letting her eyes flutter shut. "That's a good boy," she cooed, letting the older man work at her sensitive clit, tonguing her with some sense of practice from his motions.

She hunched forward a little, her heavy tits jiggling as she shuddered with each moan. She was enjoying herself, that much was easy to see. Her pleasured sounds growing louder and louder, making Adom worry that some of the Ka'reem guards might overhear and investigate.

Though when he tried to pull away, she pulled him locked back into place and continued to grind upon his face.

"I... I want you to get a message out for me," she said, her words peppered with heavy panting as her stomach tightened and her pleasure mounted. "Maybe something even more when... when we've become a little closer. More trusting."

Adom couldn't respond as he was, but he grasped her powerful thighs and did his duty to service her, flicking her clit and eating her out.

He was locked there, licking and tonguing her cunt until at last, Yvel spasmed and cried aloud. She thrust her pelvis into him, and her pussy gushed thick honey onto his face as she came.

Adom didn't find himself freed from her clutches right away though. She took her time, grinding and swiveling her hips, working out every last moment of pleasure before she finally pulled away, panting.

"Very good," she commended him curtly, her pussy lips puffy and reddened from her pleasured high.

The Ambassador licked his lips, gasping for air as he wiped about his mouth, cleaning away her juices.

"You will do these things for me, yes?" she said, tugging him by his hair to make him stand once more, sounding so deviously sexy.

"A message, yes," he said, breathing heavily, practically panting himself. "But more than that... I need to know I can trust you," he said, grasping upon the edge of the table.

"That is a start," she said with a grin.

Yvel pushed against his bare chest with her palm, guiding him to lie back upon the table. Her other hand then reached down, tugging his trousers and underpants out of the way, to let his cock stick up into the air, stiff and pulsating.

"One last thing before we part, though," she said, climbing up atop the table and straddling over him.

"What?" he asked, eyes wide as he stared up at her, entranced by her beauty, those delightfully thick tits dangling before his face.

"I need your seed inside me," she said so matter-of-factly.

Adom didn't know what to make of that, but he wasn't about to object. Not with her so near, his body burning with desire. He'd been so long without the touch of another.

He let her wrap her fingers about his cock, pump its veiny girth a few times as she lined up the purple crown with her glistening slit.

She wasted no time. In a flash, she plunged down around him, her cunt swallowing up his cock in full with one swift motion. That tight, narrow quim of hers squeezing about his girth and making him cry out noisily this time, endangering them both.

"Quiet," she hissed, striking him across the face and dazing him. "We'll both be put to death if found like this."

Knowing the rule of law in the realm of the God-King, and how protective he was over the warrior-concubines, Adom had no doubt about that.

So he kept his lips shut tight and watched as that pale beauty from the northern steppes began to ride him without easing into it at all.

She'd rise up again, sliding along his shaft, then abruptly slam back down. Gravity taking her breasts for such a ride, before they crashed back down to jiggle and bounce.

It was a hypnotizing sight to the Ambassador, who stared in awe, doing his best to keep his pleasured noises quiet.

Her tight passageway took him all in, letting his cock vanish into her womanhood as she panted. Her pace quickened with each new bounce atop him, and her narrow clench seemed focussed purely upon milking him dry.

"Cum in me," she commanded in a husky voice, so much of the sultriness gone. Now she was urgent, just wanted what she was after. "Do it. Do it now," she ordered.

Adom might've found it hard to cum on command, but the woman's tight embrace and her frenzied riding were making it an inevitability.

He tensed up, his eyes shutting as his hips up thrust in her direction, only to be battered back down each time she crashed against him.

Adom felt his balls tighten, and then in mere moments a fiery trail of pleasure was shooting up his shaft and then... there it was. Just as she demanded, he spurt his creamy seed into her depths, splattering against her fertile womb.

Yvel knew his time was come, and she ceased her riding, locking their loins together as she clenched and squeezed him dry of each last spurt. Every last droplet.

"There. There you go," she rasped, her breasts brushing against his face as she bent over him. "Good boy," she commended once more.

Moments seemed to fade out of telling for Adom, but she lingered a while, catching all he had before he regained his senses enough to speak.

"Why?" he asked meekly, still panting.

Yvel didn't answer right away.

Instead, she pulled from him, cupped her sex and kept the sloppy mess of their rutting inside her with her tightly clenched fingers.

"Why?" she repeated, crooking a brow at the man.

He nodded weakly to her as his slick, glistening cock bobbed free of her, still mostly stiff after their fucking.

"Because my choices are my own, and I will offer my virginity to the first random fool I can trust to keep it a secret before I'll give it to the God-King tonight," she said, the bitterness in her voice palpable.

Adom, however, was blown away by her words.

"Well... you can trust me," he said.

"Of course I can, fool," she bit back, her earlier fawning temperament gone. "For stealing a warrior-concubine's virginity before the God-King can claim it, you would face an end that would make death but a sweet relief."

She rolled her eyes before softening her countenance a little once more.

"Here," she said, pulling a scroll from inside her cloak and laying it down upon the table beside him. "This is what I need delivered to the Empire. Will you do this for me?" she asked sceptically.

Adom sat up wearily, pulling his trousers back around his manhood before lifting the scroll and studying it. He noted the name written upon it in Imperial common script.

His eyes widened.

"You want to send a message to—"

Yvel nodded.

"But wh—"

She held up a hand, stopping him as she began to tidy her own self up with a cloth from out of her cloak.

"Do this for me, Frenel, my darling," she said with some hint of a purr. "And then we will talk about the whys and what else you may do for me."

"Still," he said, clutching the scroll a little too tight. "This will be difficult even for me."

She nodded, seeming to only half care.

"But you will get it done. Because if there is one person who can help us with our revenge — both yours and mine — it will be her," she said, grinning deviously.

CHAPTER 12

"By overstepping, you have put me in an awkward position," came Kulav's chastising words for Mirella.

"I can't very well march off to war now with the Coven like this. Do you realize what you've done?" he demanded of her, though his voice was raised, it wasn't a yell.

Kulav looked down upon her with the stern kind of disapproval of a father more than anything else.

"I was trying to keep them from bothering you!" she objected, blurting out the obstinate denial before she could take even a moment to think about it.

"You should have used better judgment! Now I have to take time to satiate their demands instead of preparing for the battle," he said.

"You don't have to do anything if you don't want to! You're the God-King!"

"I still have to live with the political realities of being ruler, you insolent little…"

The God-King reached his limits with the obstinate woman.

Her face was still screwed up in angry defensiveness when he reached out, grasped her by the shoulder and pulled her in close.

"What are you—?!"

She didn't get a chance to finish.

He picked her up as he sat down in the oak chair of their private quarters, then without delay draped her over his knees.

"Let me go!" she demanded of him, but that was a mistake.

She knew better than to try and command the God-King around when he was already worked up.

The first strike of his palm struck her rear over her gown, but all the same it was hard enough to make her gasp and squeal.

"I'm the Queen! You can't!" she said again, immediately regretting it.

Kulav tugged up her gossamer gown, made especially for her, and then struck her rear directly. His dark skin striking upon her pale, alabaster flesh, making a resounding smack as even her skimpy panties did nothing to shield her from the blow.

"I'm your wife!" she called out, struggling in futility.

Though her objections merely earned her another strike that caused her to wail and squirm, her long nails digging into his thigh.

"You *are* my wife, but you are the wife of the God-King! Not any mere man," he growled at her in frustration, his hard hand lingering upon her stinging cheeks. "By letting your ego run wild you've backed me into a corner! I either see to the Coven's request, or I march to war, leaving you with a rebellious force that sees you as a usurper," he growled, explaining his position.

Right before landing yet another slap upon her ass cheeks that made her scream and quiver.

"I'm sorry!" she relented at last, eyes watery from the pain.

Though the apology came too late to spare her a final spank.

The God-King pulled down her panties, yanked them off her slender legs and down her ankles and feet, then struck across her fully bare ass one final, rough time. It made her cry out and sob a little, but for some reason, Mirella knew she was overdoing it a little.

In some display that was purely intended to fish for sympathy, she felt herself acting like the petulant princess had so many times over the years she tended her. Her new body was weaker than her old form, no doubt, but even she wasn't so delicate as she was behaving.

"We've got our roles in this all, Mirella," he growled, and she felt his hand reach in between her smooth inner thighs.

"If we're to succeed as rulers, you have to play your part, as I do mine," he instructed her as his fingers touched upon her sensitive slit and made her jerk in place atop his lap.

"I'm sorry, my love!" she pleaded desperately, his strong fingers touching upon her delicate flesh, making her writhe. "I don't know what's been coming over me!" she said as he stroked her slick little pussy, igniting her fires all the more.

"You've let your new position go to your head. Made you think you could act my equal for all the world," he grunted, his fingers splaying open her slit as they delved slowly in, stretching her open. "I'm very disappointed, pet. You knew better when we first met. Mirella would never embarrass us both like that."

His words stung as his fingers soothed and excited.

What he said was so true. Too true.

The Mirella she was but a year or two ago would not have dared challenge the God-King's authority like that. Let alone in public. Knowing he held her in such high esteem in private would have been enough for her, for she never sought the spotlight.

"I'll be good from now on! I swear!" she pleaded, feeling him tease her cunny hole before plucking his digits out.

"Show me you're sorry," he said, pushing his glistening fingers before her face, the scent of her honey aroma filling her nostrils.

Her glittering, wet eyes peered up at him as she reached her tongue out. Very obediently, she fought the inner urges to be disobedient and lapped at his fingers. Her motions were smooth, slowly overcoming her quivering as she obediently began to fellate his fingers.

How many times had she done this before? With an eagerness, a desire to please him more than any other? Hours she had spent, worshiping his impressive body, spending time exploring every vein, every ripple of muscle, every hard edge.

So where was this desire to revolt coming from? The desire to nip at him, to not worship, but instead tease, had not been present at the beginning of their relationship.

Kulav watched in silence, but she could feel his impressive girth prodding into her belly.

She puckered her lips around them and suckled, not letting her gaze leave his eyes as she performed for his delighted entertainment. Until finally she popped her lips free from him and murmured softly:

"I'm sorry, Your Greatness," she said in a wispy voice, batting her long, curved lashes.

"I know you are," he said, helping her stand back up, minus her panties. "But you need to keep yourself in check better from now on. Exercise self-control, pet," he cautioned her, picking up her panties.

Though instead of handing them back to her, he stuffed them into a pouch at his belt.

"I will," she said demurely, even though the fire in her loins now felt out of control and without anything to douse it.

"Now come with me," he instructed, turning and making his way toward the door.

"Where to, Your Greatness?" she asked.

"To meet with the new warrior-concubines. You are going to stand beside me as I gift them my seed," he said sternly, only a slight smirk upon his lips.

CHAPTER 13

Inside the Queen was fuming.

She'd not wanted this.

Though part of her remembered how willingly she'd aided the God-King before. How she'd lived to serve him, and was glad to help him in such acts. To watch him seed so many others, without envy or jealousy, because she knew in her heart that she had claimed a part of him never seen by another woman.

She did her best to cling to that part of herself, if only to get through the ceremony.

All around, the ceremonial chambers were lined up the young women of the warrior-concubines. Almost exclusively dark-haired, they were Ka'reem women of birth, except for the two blonde-haired Aristean women who had managed to earn their way into the ranks.

"Soon, war will be upon us all again," Kulav said, speaking to the women in his formal voice as he walked the red carpeted aisle, studying them each.

"But before any of us march off to war, I must pay you each a long-overdue visit, my warrior-concubines," he stated, undoing the clasp of his cloak and letting it slide from his shoulders.

The Queen was there behind him, ready to pull his cloak from his back as she did her best bout of acting, keeping a smile upon her face the whole time.

She just willed herself to focus upon Kulav's gloriously sculpted torso, his rippling musculature. And the words he'd said to her on the way to the private ceremony:

I was hoping to phase out these rituals. Bring an end to the ceremonies, for the time being at least. These women should be freed from their slavish devotion to me, if only because it is tiresome to me.

You, my wife, are my focus. My joy.

I tire of playing with newly minted women when the finest woman I have ever met serves me loyally already. Who makes me yearn to haul her into the blighted north and rut endlessly in a cave, just her and I.

Of course, all of that had followed with not just his plan but his cautionary words as well:

But I am more than a mere man or husband. I am the future ruler of all, and you shall serve me as every other being upon the face of this planet is destined to. Whether it is upon your knees, back, or with your words.

It sent a shiver down Mirella's spine, just thinking of the rough tone of voice he said it with.

The absolute certainty of it all. But she'd known that from the beginning, and celebrated it along with him.

"Soon you will all be entrusted with a momentous task. One which shall yet again decide the future of my people, my nation," he said, touring along in front of each woman.

None dared meet his eyes of course, that is, until they came to one woman in particular.

Tall, even by Ka'reem standards, she had obsidian hair and a thick mane, a glint to her eyes as her half-smile gave her a sly sort of look.

Kulav stopped to study her a moment, her breasts exposed, held along on a silver-chained brazier. He took his liberties with her, reaching out and cupping a large breast, squeezing it for his pleasure as the two continued to stare.

Mirella didn't know how to react.

No, that was a lie.

She knew the proper course: silence. Wait and let him handle things as she draped his cloak over her slender forearm.

Kulav took his time, but when he was done, he walked away from the woman, leaving her with flushed cheeks, stiff teats and a less smug expression.

Mirella remembered back to something that Kulav had said to her so many years ago, when she first met with him for the ritual:

"Other women are offered up to me, but even they cringe in fear of me. Fear what they shall birth, no matter how much their loved ones talk of the honour and privilege."

The tall woman did not cringe in fear, and Mirella's hair stood on end. She'd been special to him because of her strange treatment of the God-king. But what if there was another like her? Another who did not fear his wrath but embraced it?

"Disrobe," he commanded them all, and they undid the clasps of their own raven cloaks as he moved to the center of the room.

Mirella walked in behind him, placing his own cloak aside as she reached around his waist and began to undo his leather pants. Her nimble fingers quickly opened them, though peeling away the tight garment took more force.

All eyes travelled to him, in various degrees of sheepishness as his thick cock rose out of his trousers, pulsating with bulging veins. It was without a doubt the largest any of them had seen, pushing out proudly above his thick, muscular thighs.

Once his pants were removed, Kulav stepped out of them and walked towards the first woman on his right.

"Bend over," he commanded with a voice of simple authority.

She complied immediately, turning and bending over the stone altar that was once a religious symbol.

"Part your legs wider," he instructed the woman.

She splayed her thighs open wide, her anklets tinkling as she planted her feet apart.

He didn't take the woman right then, however, as all eyes watched he nodded to the Queen, and wordlessly, she did her duty.

Dressed in her see-through gown, she reached around him, her dainty fingers wrapping about his thick cock as best they could. It took both hands to work his manhood effectively, but she began to pump the full length of his cock.

The God-King had little use for restraint. He simply grunted and moaned as his wife and Queen worked upon his organ.

Kulav shut his eyes, hands rested upon his hips as she worked him to the point of release.

Then, without delay, he reached out and took hold of the warrior-concubine's hips, and the Queen guided him into her waiting cunny. Just barely.

Her hands continued to work along his length as his balls tightened and his cock disgorged thick jets of his seed, filling the aspiring woman's womb.

Fulfilling his duty to her.

Just like that, he pulled out and moved to the next woman.

"Bend over," he commanded of her.

The once debauched and spontaneous visits to his harem had become something ritualized. Formal.

Another woman bent over to join the other that still waited in position, not being told to rise, but still trembling in desirous awe.

King and Queen repeated their actions, more of her quick pumping that strained her dainty wrists and made her fingers hurt, but she worked him with flair and expertise, twisting her wrists as she pumped his length.

It took longer the second time, but the time eventually came, and he pushed himself into the waiting initiate, blowing a load of his seed into her as well.

On it went, though as soon as the next woman was bent over, Kulav gave a look to Mirella and indicated downwards with a mere flicker of his eyes.

The dutiful Queen fell to her knees, and instead of merely working her hands upon him, this time she put her mouth to use. Lips and tongue paid reverence to the God-King's mighty spear, lavishing attention upon its full length, from base to tip.

The end result was the same, of course. As his deep, husky moans grew to the point of release, he pushed his tip into the next woman and filled her loins with his seed as well.

It wasn't the wild, passionate claiming of previous years when the God-King took his concubines, but it was debauched in a whole other way. This was a ritual claiming of woman after woman, with the subservient Queen servicing her King at the altar of each woman's body.

Of course, the more Mirella did it, the less her anger broiled within her.

She was subservient before her King as she sucked and licked upon his cock, but each time she asserted herself over the woman he claimed. She marked herself as above each of them. A go-between for the King and his subjects. A priestess for the God.

When it came time for the final woman, the defiant one who dared to look her King in the eyes, Kulav paused.

He took his time looking her over once more.

The silence in the air was palpable, as he'd left in his wake a room full of cum-dribbling cunts.

But he brushed back his thick dark hair and wiped the light perspiration from his brow.

Mirella awaited whatever punishment he had in store for the brazen woman, a quiet, hidden glee within her.

"You. You shall serve outside my quarters over the coming days. I shall claim you when it pleases me," he said before turning and walking back to the center of the room to reclaim his things.

Mirella was stunned. A sickness came to her stomach, a prickling heat overtaking her face that she prayed the other women couldn't see.

No. Her heart fell in her chest, her fears coming to pass.

Mirella sluggishly followed after him to pick up his things and help redress him as he spoke.

"The rest of you, arise and claim your rightful position. You are among the chosen ones, and your legacy is now mixed with mine for all of history yet to be made."

Their shouting roar filled the room, each of the women excited by his words, even if the claiming had not been what they were told to expect.

However, Mirella and the defiant woman stood apart, quietly contemplating different matters of the God-King. And what his words meant for them in particular.

CHAPTER 14

To be given a position of any sort by the God-King was no insult, Mirella knew that much.

So seeing him instruct the brazen woman to serve outside their quarters that evening and await his instructions just grated upon her all the more.

That rebellious part of her wouldn't let it go.

Even as the carriage rode on down over the cobblestones through the streets of Ariste, her friend beside her.

"Your Majesty?" Svella asked, concern in her voice as she reached over to touch upon Mirella's arm.

"Sorry Svella," she said, tearing her gaze away from the window and brushing back her blonde hair.

"You were off in another plane of existence," Svella remarked, an amused smile upon her face.

The Queen laughed and toyed with her necklace idly, already finding herself getting lost in thought again.

"Just caught up in thoughts about… everything," she lied, if only a little. Mainly, her mind kept trying to pull her back to worries and jealousies.

"I've noticed you have been like that since I returned, Your Majesty," Svella said.

"Please, call me Mirella when we're alone. It… reminds me of who I really am. I need that more and more, I think," the Queen lamented, the words striking her truer when said aloud then she realized they were.

Svella studied her with some concern showing upon her furrowed brow.

"There is something wrong. Something serious," Svella pointed out.

"Just this coming war," Mirella objected.

Svella stared at her a while but acquiesced with a nod as her concerned expression faded from her face.

"Very well, sister. What do you have in mind for the coming battle?"

Mirella felt relieved that the topic of discussion had shifted back to pure duty.

"We must gather up the city's masons and make sure the outer walls are shored up for the coming siege. They've not been tended to as closely as they were since the God-King claimed the city his own, and we don't want them failing us in the midst of a siege."

"Of course, Mirella. I will have the sisters gather up the masons for that every task."

"But let's be kind about it, Svella," the Queen said. "They are subjects of the God-King now, not cattle. Let's treat them as we would the Ka'reem. Or as close as you can manage."

Svella chuckled, and for a brief moment the Queen felt her stomach knot, but it went away.

"I am not so sure they could handle such treatment, Mirella, but I get your point," Svella said with a wry smile, seeming to enjoy the idea a great deal. "Can you imagine the Aristeans engaging in the Blood Ceremony? Or running across the snowy winter plains in the nude for the Moon Tide?"

Mirella laughed, but frankly, she could barely imagine it herself. Up until she'd done the latter, at least, as part of a holiday ceremony shortly after the God-King united both the peoples of the steppes and the city.

"You might as well tell them to walk on their hands down the road, Svella," Mirella said, smiling out the window as they travelled on through the streets in their carriage.

"The sister's numbers are greater than ever now, Mirella. We even have some select few Aristean women who have risen up to join our ranks. I never thought I'd see the day," Svella remarked wistfully.

"Me either," she said, feeling a pang of jealousy as she remembered the one at the ceremony with Kulav.

The constant sensations of jealousy and frustrating outbursts were beginning to overwhelm her. They weren't her actions at all, but like a voice of some other creature, egging her on to self-sabotage. Undermining all she had accomplished.

She daren't think of who they belong to, the fear too great.

"Are you alright?" Svella asked, reaching out to touch upon her shoulder.

In her frustration, the Queen had bent and clutched her head, but the moment Svella's hand made contact with her she jerked away and snapped.

"Don't touch me, peasant!" she snarled, eyes filled with anger, breathing heavy.

Svella slowly recoiled and stared at her in silent confusion.

It took the Queen a moment to climb down from that strange place and realize the implications of her actions.

"I'm so sorry, Svella," she backpedaled, reaching out to touch her friend's arm. "I don't… I don't know what came over me. It's like… like I'm losing my mind lately."

Mirella's lower lip quivered, and Svella's brow furrowed. There was more honesty in that statement than she'd said in months.

What offense the Ka'reem woman took was pushed aside as she reached out and embraced her comrade, wrapping her into her arms and holding her to her bosom. Silence overtaking them for a while as they rode along.

"What's happening to me, Svella?" Mirella said, feeling so weak and confused then.

A pause permeated the air, with Svella not knowing the right thing to say. Or how to say what she thought. Until at last, she spoke again. "I know not for certain, my friend," she remarked, stroking her fingers over Mirella's hair, "but it is nothing you can't handle. I *am* certain of that."

CHAPTER 15

When the God-King emerged from his residence, Yvel was quick to rise from her seat outside his door. Her posture was crisp and tall, her ample bosom out as she smiled, looking all too pleased with the position she was given.

"How may I service you, Your Greatness?" she asked in a sultry purr, holding none of her charm back as she presented her generous assets through her open cloak.

"Come with me," he ordered with little delay, leading her on down a corridor of the private, royal section of the palace where few servants ever wandered.

Yvel was a tall woman with a long stride, but even still it took some effort to keep up with the God-

King's pace. Yet another of the many ways he excelled all those around him.

Truth be told, despite her resentment, Yvel was having a hard time not finding herself in awe of the God-King.

To hear tale of him was one thing, but to walk in his path, to gaze up at his strikingly handsome face, or over his broad, powerful body... Yvel was thrown off by him. All her plans suddenly seeming so... secondary.

She fought that however, as best she could. But her primary goal, despite herself, had become to earn the favour of the God-King, to impress this epitome of manhood.

"Thank you for your attentions, Your Greatness," she said, walking beside him, still dressed in her ceremonial garb that left so little to the imagination beneath her cloak. And made her breasts bounce awkwardly as she moved.

She got no response from him, but that only made her want to push more for the satisfaction of his acknowledgment that she sought.

"I have always been the pride of my group, wherever I've gone," she said, trying not to boast but finding herself so moved to sway him she did so anyhow. "And I aim to impress you similarly if I can. The God-King deserves only the best, and only my best."

She felt foolish immediately after having said it, but when it earned a look over his broad shoulders at her, she couldn't help but smile up at him broadly. Loving even that brief bit of attention.

They continued on for some time through the winding halls of the palace, until at last they came to a door of one of the chambers.

"Wait here," he commanded before disappearing inside.

Yvel obeyed with a crisp, "Yes, Your Greatness".

Though once the door shut, she pressed her back to the wall and let out a heavy sigh.

She felt like a foolish girl, the sort she'd never been before.

As much as she'd felt special to be singled out in the ceremony, her cunny had been set to throbbing with a need ever since. Her moisture leaving her inner thighs awkwardly damp as she awaited the God-King's next orders.

Despite her attempts to keep calm, pressing her back to the cool stone of the wall, she found herself giving into temptation.

Her fingers slid along her taut tummy, down over her mons and through the bed of hair above her cunny.

From her position, she could only hear the low rumble of the God-King's voice in the other room, but that was all she needed to help make the fantasy come alive in her mind.

Yvel didn't often touch herself, but there, standing in the palace hallway, she began to finger her slit and let her digits dance upon her sensitive clit. She whimpered, and that noise made her worry.

She promised herself that she'd not touch upon that sensitive bundle of nerves directly again as she stood there, she just... she just had to get a little relief.

Just a few more teasing touches upon her pussy as she imagined the thickly muscled God-King claiming her.

That big, broad man pressing her up against the wall and claiming her, then and there.

Not cold and perfunctory like the other women in the ceremonial hall, but passionate. Hard.

She could visualize and almost feel him lifting her up and splaying her legs open, plunging that immense, obsidian shaft right up into her, making her scream out loud!

Somehow she'd missed the sound of the door opening up, because when she fluttered her eyes open she was mortified to see that the God-King stood there, watching her.

His looming presence soaking in the lewd sight of her fingering herself and twisting upon her nipple in thoughts of him.

Her cheeks burned red with embarrassment as she stood beneath his steely gaze.

The God-King didn't look cold so much as just… studious. Looking her over with intense interest.

Yvel didn't know how to take that however, and only after a delay did she slowly trail her slick fingers up over her belly toward her breasts, leaving a gleaming trail. She bit down upon her lower lip and looked him over, thinking she detected a stirring there in his loins.

"Retire for now," he commanded abruptly, in his deep, husky voice. "Then you will attend to me this evening. Be waiting."

With that, the God-King turned and left, his cloak sweeping behind him.

Though Yvel could only think of how sweet that evening would be, and her excitement began to overwhelm her as she ground her thighs together to still the incessant throb.

CHAPTER 16

Things were moving so quickly, that the last day had felt like a month to Mirella.

It's not that there had been so many things happening compared to her usual hectic schedule, but the anxiety of preparing for war once again, compounded with the grief and her own issues left Mirella feeling... overwhelmed.

Just walking the halls on her way to her next engagement had become her sole reprieve, her only moment of relaxation.

Yet despite her inner turmoil and her struggle to think of what was to come, she was alert enough to notice the presence of her husband and ruler.

Up above on one of the balconies, he stood, overseeing some of the soldiers' training in the courtyard below.

Mirella smiled a little and made her way inside, winding up the staircase before she came up behind Kulav as quietly as she could manage.

"Your footsteps are so light, even in those heels you wear," he remarked, his eyes remaining upon the troops training below.

"Yet you heard me all the same, your Greatness," she said, coming up behind him, touching her hand to his shoulder blade as she came to stand beside him.

"I can feel you before I ever hear you, my precious," he said, his full lips spreading into a broad smile at her. Though even his loving warmth couldn't fully hide his pain then.

"You miss her so dearly," Mirella said, reaching her hand up from his shoulder to cup his cheek, stroking along his jawline. "I am so sorry, my love," she said sweetly, looking up at her lover with such sympathy in her eyes.

Kulav's gaze dipped away, off at nothing in particular as he let her touch upon his face.

"I knew it was coming for so long. Yet even still… it felt as if a sudden shock to me." He shook his head solemnly. "I did my best to push it out of my mind, hoping she would recover. She didn't need to go so soon."

Mirella's brow furrowed, and she continued to pet his cheek, feeling his strong jaw bone, soothing the worried lines from his face.

"There was nothing more to do. Nothing anyone could have done. You sent for healers from across the world, and none of them were able to reverse what she knowingly took upon herself," Mirella comforted.

"What she took upon herself for me," he said through gritted teeth, his hands squeezing the marble railing before him tightly as the frustration built.

"You didn't ask her to make that sacrifice, certainly not knowing the consequences. She knew what she was doing, Kulav. And she did it for her most beloved. Her son," she comforted from atop her tip-toes, trying to pull his face down to kiss him.

The God-King resisted until finally, he gave in and wrapped his arms about her, those thick muscles squeezing her feminine form as their lips met in a passionate lock. It wasn't the fiery passion of desire, but of a need, an emotional need between man and woman that was so intensely primal.

He was a man of intense power and self-control, and she was his conduit to feel. To feel things he could never allow himself to openly display. That nobody but her would truly understand.

She was his wife, his confidant.

On the most primal of levels, she was his mate.

And that reality triumphed over all else, over all her doubts and inner-conflicts as of late, and they surrendered themselves to the warmth of passion for one another.

It was the way of Kulav and his people to not be bashful about matters of sex and sensuality, but for once he broke their kiss and looked to her.

"Come to our quarters," he said, and she knew he felt exposed out there. The mighty God-King wanted her all to himself, in privacy and seclusion, that they might connect emotionally beyond prying eyes.

"Of course, my love," she said, smiling up at him, squeezing his hand and stroking his pronounced jawline.

Kulav didn't lead her there, though, he scooped her up and carried her.

And why not? His Queen was little more than a feather's weight to his powerful arms, and his long strides took them to their destination so quickly.

Mirella nestled in against his chest, snaking one of her own slender limbs about his neck as she kissed at his chest, her pouty lips landing soft little puckered smacks upon his dark skin.

It was easy for her to feel her usual self in his grasp, able to feel his powerful sinew carrying her in security and comfort. It was there where she felt most like her old self, giving herself over to the care and affection of her lover.

The only man who had ever made her wish to willingly submit to another.

She was even able to block out the sight of that upstart young warrior-concubine who had dared to meet the God-King's gaze during the ceremony, and been offered a special position. Mirella stayed in his arms until they were past her and the guards, and back into the security of their private room.

Kulav laid her out upon the bed, took his time to gaze upon her. Soak her all in.

He had suffered a great loss, and Mirella could read in his gaze the significance of his lengthy inspection.

He wanted to appreciate her, savour her, for all she was to him. Not take for granted the woman he had met in that opulent palace one dark and tumultuous night.

"I love you, dear Mirella. With a fire that would not be quenched upon all of this city, the Empire, and the world beyond, do I love you," he professed, raising her hand to his lips and kissing softly upon her pale digits.

In those moments, all her fears and doubt, her jealous bouts, slipped away. There was no questioning the truth or the passion behind his words, the real emotion that bound them.

It seemed so silly to her, then, feeling betrayed simply because he'd given another brazen woman a special position.

In the early days of their relationship, he'd taken on so many lovers in so many manners, but he always came back to her. He had access to the most beautiful women in the lands, ceremony requiring them save themselves for him, and yet he'd come to her.

Even when she was already pregnant, he broke with all social taboo, and took her again and again.

It was wrong in the eyes of her sisters to spill the God-King's seed fruitlessly in an already pregnant womb, but it didn't stop either of them from doing so and enjoying it.

For years he'd stayed with her, at her side despite the many changes to him, to her, to the land. Their lives had been through upheaval, and they remained one another's rock.

Her finger grazed against his lip, feeling her soft pad caress his rougher skin, and in that blissful moment, it was just them, as they were. Still passionately in love.

Her mouth found his, their warmth combining as she pressed in against him, her body delicately posed on the bed.

"My King. My Lord," she murmured, her pale blue eyes hidden behind her translucent eyelids, "My God."

She was not entirely the woman she once was, her shift in bodies made sure of that. But in the moment, beneath Kulav's great, dark, muscle rippling body, she felt like her old self.

And he felt just as glorious ever.

Her fingers searched out over his rippling abs, his chiseled pecs. She could feel the veined bulges of his biceps as he clutched her close, the power that lay coiled in those thick arms of his.

His large hands began to peel away her gossamer gown, stripping off that sheer fabric to reveal her pink flesh beneath. Then they moved to cup her breasts, squeezed those two mounds as their lips noisily smacked together.

She'd given him everything she had, become so much stronger than she was in the past, all in dedication and in service to him. Found a peace and a purpose, a strength born of her devotion and pure love.

The haunting last words of Kulav's mother came to her, unbidden.

You and I can only sacrifice what is ours to give, Mirella… take care of my son.

The memory further solidified her need to be herself, to give in to what their relationship was. To trust herself in his arms.

Her pink nipples stiffened beneath his dark skin, her flesh turning a heated colour as her loins burned with desire. She'd watched him seed so many concubines, but it was nothing like what they had.

Her warlord lover became worked to a frenzy, his hard hands groping at her flesh with such hunger, such desire.

His passionate lips kissed down from hers, across her slender neck as she turned her head to the side. He tugged her dress down further as his mouth moved across her collarbones, then to devour her stiffened teats.

Those mounds of breast flesh were already so much thicker, fuller than when she'd first claimed her new body. Pregnancy, she believed, was to bear the blame for that.

Though with how her husband kissed, suckled and devoured those mounds he only seemed to appreciate their fuller nature, and how they more resembled her old self.

Her dress came down to her hips, exposing her stomach, letting his fingers roam over her smooth, taut belly, fully recovered from her last birth. And her lover gave a growl of desire.

That sound reverberated through her and her body ached for his touch, the feel of his rough tongue and lips clasped around her making her eyes roll back.

Her fingers reached for his arms, clutching onto him and writhing beneath him with such desire.

"My love," she cooed in her sweet, youthful voice, sullied by lust. "There's only ever you in my life. The one I breathe for."

Kulav squeezed her body in his hands, clenching her hip and breast as he continued to kiss down her body, moving from her glistening, stiff nipples.

There, above her womanhood, he paused, inhaling her scent as he tugged her gown down, freeing her of the last of her clothing. He revelled in her aroma, his nostrils flaring, his manhood rising, and he rubbed his palms over her thighs, spreading them back as he stared down at her.

"It is not a thing even a God-King can ask of a woman," he said in his gravelly husk, letting his thumbs trail in along her inner thighs, "but my love… how I wish I could plant a daughter in you. And carry my mother's legacy in her name and upbringing."

She shivered, the words and their meaning coursing through her veins, impacting her in a way that so little could. She knew how much that meant for him to say, and her stomach clenched. Arousal and sentiment swirled within her, teased her body to such erotic highs.

"She was so proud of you," Mirella whispered, her eyes shut, giving her the comfort of darkness.

Kulav took in a deep breath, and though he didn't release a sigh, she could feel the tension in him.

He exercised it in other ways, though, and his large hands reached to his waist, worked open his belt and trousers, pulling them down to unveil his pulsating shaft.

Mirella's eyes could not help but open then, to witness the thick, ebon girth that — despite the eventful day — swelled and throbbed with desire for her. And her alone. With no other concubines or play things to split his fancy with.

He shed them both of all their clothes and bent down over her, letting the slab of his cock smack against her moist slit.

His lips kissed at her chest and moved up, retracing his previous steps back to her mouth.

"And the most important thing she did of all after giving birth to me, was to lead me to you, my sweet wife," he said in a deep husk, stroking a hand back over her blonde hair.

Mirella's lips pressed against him with such need and passion, her little tongue flicking against his as her fingers found his cock. It was so unlike earlier in the day, which had been so detached. So formal.

This time he was heated, throbbing with not just a primal urge, but with lust.

Her fingers wrapped around his shaft, but she didn't urge him in. Instead, she felt along his veins, holding him with renewed appreciation for his hefty tool.

Their loins pressed together, hers slick and ready, his hard and throbbing. They savoured the moment of closeness before it became pure carnality, holding and touching one another, letting all else but the two of them fade away, slip out of reality, out of recognition. To seem as unimportant as it truly was in the face of their love and desire.

Their tongues swirled, lashed and danced together, and Kulav felt up her body, squeezed her sensitive breasts once more. Nipped at her lower lip, tugged it. Bit it.

"I only wish fate would let us travel together on this journey ahead, my love… the long nights ahead without you shall be made miserable by your absence," he said, rocking his hips just a bit at first, as instinct took over his motions.

Her free hand found his firm ass, squeezing it as she contorted her body to meet his. Her legs spread, her flower offered upon his swollen crown, and still they savoured the moment.

"The nights are dark without you," she murmurs breathily. "But I will hold onto *this* night for all of those nights duty requires you elsewhere."

Their eyes met then, in a brief moment of understanding and devotion, just before his thick cock speared down into her. That throbbing shaft stretching her pink cunny open wide, splaying her slick lips about his immense girth.

Kulav gave a deeply satisfied moan as he dipped down into her depths, one unlike anything he ever gave the concubines that ritual pressed upon him.

And to watch him, the pleasure was undeniable with how his masculine features contorted. His muscles tensed and bulged.

Her legs tightened around him, beckoning him in despite his heft and impressive size. It was obscene, and yet she desired him so. To feel nothing but his body all around her, inside her, claiming her for his own once more.

No time was lost, for once passions were unfurled, they were lost in their lust.

Kulav slid one hand along her leg, lifted it up to his hip, and began to piston his thick shaft down into her. It was slow at first, but hard, and only grew more intense as he built speed.

Their lips smacked and he fondled her breast with his free hand, his thick thighs and calves supporting him as he took her atop their marital bed.

The God-King had made love to her so many, many times, against tradition, with it, every way in between. But knowing he would soon be apart from her made the moment all the more intense for them both, and Kulav moaned with pleasure between the moist smacks of their lips.

They'd been together for so long, kept close to home to rule over the kingdom. And the last time he had left her, they nearly lost everything.

Both of them knew that well, and it only added kindling to the fire that already burned so bright between them.

"Oh!" moaned Mirella, her spine contorting as she pressed her chest to his hand, let him explore her with his rough fingers. It ached between her thighs, each hard thrust bringing her closer to her own inevitable orgasm.

The mighty Kulav fucked her harder, his heavy balls slapping against her ass as he built pace, loosened her tight quim to accommodate his girth.

That dark chest of his gleamed with perspiration in the dim light as they rut, the sturdy bed groaned, and Kulav grunted.

Each swell of his shaft made her cunny twinge with the raw size of his manhood, but she took him, even savoured him, where other women might've cringed and wilted at his roughness and size.

"In the long nights ahead," he said, his voice peppered with his heaving breaths, "I shall cling to the memory of your tight embrace... your glorious body."

He pinched one of her nipples between his thumb and index finger, tortured that poor, pink peak as he looked her over and licked at his full lips.

She cried out at that, her body so desperate for that all-encompassing release. She craved it almost as much as she craved his body, for him to find pleasure in hers.

"Kulav!" she cried out, her body trembling as that familiar sensation violently spread from her stomach, jolting through her legs and arms, making her cling to him with such passion.

Her whole body tensed about him, but he never relented.

The conqueror of nations claimed her body long ago, and he did so again. Thrusting roughly into her as her cunny clenched his girth, making him moan in turn.

He only pounded her harder, more intensely, squeezed and groped at her tender teats and bucked his hips.

Her pale form against his dark skin made for such beautiful artistry.

The Demon-King, as he was known in the empire down south, so stunningly gorgeous. The perfect male specimen, and there she was, wrapped about his gloriously immense cock, feeling her limbs tingle with electric pleasure.

Her heels dug into his ass, coaxing herself to higher and higher peaks as he forced her to shudder with every earth-shattering pound of his body against hers.

Her mind went blissfully quiet, leaving only her and him, and the passion and affection that bound them in that moment.

She gushed slick, warm honey over his loins, coating his balls so that they slapped against her rear with such a wet, loud smack.

He was ravenous for her, and he squeezed her thigh and breast tighter, harder, letting his fingers move up from her tits to her neck.

"I am going to seed your womb and mark it mine once more," he growled out gruffly.

His dick swelled and expanded inside her erratically, wildly! And she knew his time was nearing its end too. That he couldn't hold off the pleasure for much longer.

Especially with how her tight little pussy squeezed him, pulsing as pleasure travelled from her to him.

"Yes," she pleaded with him, her voice desperate and airy. "Yes, my King!"

She watched through narrow slits as his broad-shouldered body arched back, the entirety of his bulging muscles on display as they twitched and moved. All that gorgeous sinew rippling beneath his smooth, ebon skin put to work plowing his manhood into her, feeling her flesh and thrusting hard.

His broad-jawed face was locked in a look of ecstasy, but before he would allow himself to reach his peak… he took his time with her once more.

His thumb reached in from her thigh, teased her clit, running circles about it, pressing upon the sensitive bud.

"Cum upon my cock… do as your King commands," he husked his demand.

She was already so sensitive, and that hard digit pressing against her most tender of places elicited a jolt through her system. Her cunny pulsed, squeezing him tighter in her carnal grasp, but he didn't relent.

Nor did he pause when her leg spasmed, kicking him with her heel as she bucked and jerked beneath his mighty weight.

Only when she screamed his name, her entire body reverberating and completely lost to pure bliss, did he give in himself.

The mighty God-King brought to a shuddering finale with her flesh. *Within* her flesh.

His eyes shut and he slid his hands up along her legs as he let loose such a roar that carried through the palace halls.

He bucked and tensed, his whole body moving to his pleasured sensations as he flooded her fertile depths with his rich, copious seed.

Thick jets of that creamy cum punctuating each thrust, filling her womb with its virility.

And she thought on his words... on how deeply the loss of his mother affected him, on how much it would mean to give this man — her husband, her King, her God — a daughter. And even as pleasure hazed her mind and distracted her, she focussed all her willpower.

All her inner strength.

Focussed it all upon giving him what he wanted. Upon using her new body to be the receptacle for his first daughter.

Kulav bent over her at last, as the final spurts of his seed filled her, and he kissed at her lips lovingly. The tender smacks of their passion a final, meandering end to their passionate ride.

CHAPTER 17

Yvel felt snubbed.

And that rankled her more than most anything.

The God-King had invited her to wait outside his quarters for the evening, but then he sweeps on past her with his wife in arms, ignoring her very presence and ditching her to stand, without instruction.

She continued to stand wait, balling her fists and grinding her teeth in irritation for hours.

There she was, ready and eager. Willing to toss aside her allegiance to the renegade sisters and their plans just to be with the God-King, but he would have nothing to do with her.

It was just as they said. He was made soft by the manipulations of that little princess.

There she was left, standing with a seductive smile, thinking her time had come as the God-King strode on by. Leaving her there, in her skimpy outfit, exposed, wanting… rejected.

"You're relieved," said one of the guards, come to take the position from her, as if she were no more than a mere guard to stand duty by his door.

Yvel didn't even say a word to her relief, she merely stormed off through the palace, only one thing on her mind: petty revenge.

It's what brought her out into the streets of Ariste, carried her footsteps down to the former Imperial Embassy.

Still, even in her rage she took caution, and approached the place through a back window, not watched as closely by the guards that were positioned to keep an eye upon the ambassador.

Since the God-King took control of Ariste, the nights were ever quiet except for in times of celebration. His guards kept the streets safe and clean through a tightly enforced curfew. Though of course, someone like Yvel was exempt from a curfew, and she used it to her advantage to slip about in the darkness.

She pulled herself up to the second story window as she'd done the time before, leveraging herself off the stone wall behind, the wood portcullis that covered it up sliding out of the way with only a soft grinding noise.

In just a mere moment she was pulling herself inside, though she didn't get any time to breathe after the exertion, because the sound of a strained bowstring filled the silence of the manor.

She struggled to look up at the source, but it was so dark. She could barely make out the silhouette of the man holding the crossbow upon the stairs. Only then it was made possible through the candle light coming from the bedroom above.

"It's me, you fool," she hissed into the darkness.

Adom hesitated, not wanting to lower his weapon in his paranoid state.

"Yvel," she hissed again, her frustration growing.

"How can I be sure?" he asked, his voice low and huskier than usual.

"Is this how you treat a woman you screw?" she asked contemptuously.

At last, Adom dropped the weapon, and a suppressed sigh of relief was palpable.

"Sorry, Yvel. I have been rather... tense, of late," he explained.

"Of course you have been, your time is ticking away here," she said, rising up to full height, then slowly ascending the stairs towards him.

"Do you have news to tell me?" he asked, anxiously. "Are they coming for me?"

It was hard not to notice the tension in his words, the Ambassador's life held in the palm of the God-King's hand, merely waiting to be squashed at his whim.

Yvel stepped up right beside him, however, touching her hand to his stomach and shoulder.

"Not yet," she whispered. "Did you get my message out?" she asked.

He hesitated a moment, pondering whether to be honest or not.

"Not yet," he replied in kind, but then raised a hand to silence her irritated response. "The message goes out in the morning with dawn. There are set times for this, I can't just alter that without great risks."

Yvel tensed at his response but then softened again, pressing her ample bosom up against the man's shoulder and arm. She stroked his stomach lower as she murmured into his ear.

"I have a plan I'd like to discuss with you… in greater detail," she said.

Adom looked at her in the dim light, studying the fierce Ka'reem woman to understand her curious behaviour.

After a mere moment he licked his lips and gestured back up the stairs.

"We can discuss it some more in my room. Upon my bed, if you like," he said smoothly, despite his nervousness.

Yvel laughed in amusement at the idea, her eyes sparkling in the candle light as they ascended the stairs, all despite the bitter frustration that still festered beneath the surface.

"How quaint. Fucking atop a bed," she said as she led Adom back to his room.

CHAPTER 18

The sun shone down over Ariste as countless banners fluttered from rooftops, windows, and the city walls. The God-King's colours presented everywhere about, even out into the fields where troops unnumbered awaited his commands.

It was another grand farewell for the Kingdom's ruler. Though Mirella felt dreadful about it.

The night before had been a brief but sweet return to her usual self, where Kulav and she could just be each other again, without anyone or anything interfering with that. Or with who she was.

The inner conflict that made her head feel like a noisy council chamber at times had stilled, and she found peace in her lover's arms.

Already she could feel the conflict rising again within her, and she'd not even said goodbye to her husband. It made her blind to the beauty of the city below, Kulav's countless banners in her mind slowly becoming replaced with visions of flames in the darkness.

Like the night I lost control of my own nation…

Svella came up beside her atop the grand balcony overseeing the main courtyard below.

"An important day for the history of our people," Svella said, standing just to the Queen's right, next to the alabaster stonework of the railing.

The Queen felt a twinge of anger in her for the woman's presence, or no… her words. But she pushed them down, willed herself to be *herself*. The woman she was, that had won the heart of a God-King.

"My heart pangs for his loss, Svella," Mirella lamented, finding comfort in her nude honesty with her friend.

"He shall not be lost to you or us. Merely gone for a time to tasks needing done," she reassured with a warm voice. Though in front of all the soldiers and officials she didn't follow up the comforting words with a fond hand or touch.

"I know, my friend. But I fear that without him I will lose more of myself to what… to what I'm becoming," she said, wringing her hands but otherwise trying not to betray her emotional state. Any sign of weakness in her would be seen as an ill omen.

A sign of lack of confidence in her King.

"You are in control of yourself, Mirella," came Svella's soothing voice, gone the rough edges of the warrior woman she was in her life's role. "Never before did I see someone grow so strong and in control right before my eyes, as I saw in you. This shall only be another trial among many that you shall overcome."

Mirella's full lips spread into a touched smile, and she felt her eyes become a bit glossy, but she bit back the tears. Such a thing would not be appropriate for the Queen of the Ka'reem.

"Thank you, Svella," she murmured softly, standing there in her gossamer gown as the winds blew it about on their mountain perch.

"I think... I think I would feel much more me if I could wear my old regalia," Mirella said, looking aside at Svella's raven-feather raiment, like she once wore. "I felt like I belonged here when I could wear the God-King's regalia."

"That is because you earned it, Your Majesty," Svella said with a smile. "But that was in another life, as far as most are concerned, and they would not recognize it. Not yet at least. But time will offer opportunities. You were the first woman from outside of the Ka'reem to become a true sister, after all. You can do it again."

The Queen rankled a little.

I shouldn't have to earn it again, I should just decree it so and take it, said a voice in her head.

The sun was only rising then, the fire of the sun's crest lighting the horizon on fire and glinting off the stonework city below. It was beautiful, and the metallic dyes used in the God-King's banners reflected it strikingly, as well.

His presence became apparent as the massive, dark man strode up beside Mirella, placing his hand upon her shoulder and grounding her once more.

"There was a time you could never have kept pace with me," Kulav said to Mirella in a deep, dark voice. "Now look at what you accomplish before the day has even truly been set to begin."

Mirella took the compliment to heart. She had risen early to add some flair to the God-King's departure, seeing to the distribution of more banners, the rousing of the minstrels, and gaining the attention of the people who would line up along the streets to witness their King march off to war again.

"Thank you, your Greatness," she said with a fond smile, calmed by his touch and presence. Savouring it while it lasted.

Truth be told, she did feel it was a great thing. One of the positive improvements to come from her changing self.

All her life, rising early had been forced upon her, and she loathed it. And even when that was done, and it was voluntary, she still begrudged it and couldn't keep pace with Kulav.

She'd spent the night before willing herself to wake and be ready well before sunrise to prepare the God-King's fanfare on his departure. And she didn't even feel the least bit restive or fatigued.

A miracle when it came to Mirella's disposition.

"To find you rising with me, energetic and fine, was a treat I did not expect to get this departure. I could not thank you enough for it, my love," he said in a confessional tone, his voice low. "The rest, this pageantry? Icing."

Mirella smiled up at him, her own hair beautifully coiffed in a style that combined both Aristean metropolitan standards of perfection, and the Ka'reem's love of natural, chaotic beauty.

Her blond tresses were done in an elaborate updo, but then came back around to flow over her slender shoulders, garnished with wild field-lilies from the northern steppes.

"The one and only true God-King should never set out to war without a great deal of pageantry. Your people must celebrate you in all things, most of all, your conquests. Both of the past and to come," she said, slipping down fluidly to her knees and kissing the back of his hand in homage to him, signalling the start of the whole send-off.

The trumpeters started in Aristean style, then the horns of the Ka'reem sounded. The two sounds were so dissonant and alien to one another, but somehow together they managed to produce something beautifully unique.

There would be no speeches, the ride to war would be serious. All but wordlessly grim.

Kulav guided Mirella back to her standing position, and then, with their hands still enjoined, he raised their fists into the air. In concert with their rulers, the armed forces before them raised their fists in the dawn light.

The trumpets and horns sounded, and then once Kulav lowered his fist they chanted his name. Just once, but it thundered off the mountain sides all the same.

Kulav led Mirella back into the palace to move along the stairs and out into the courtyard itself, but the Queen was instantly distracted by the presence of that upstart warrior-concubine.

"My love," Kulav said, pointing to Yvel as she waited stiffly, silently. "While I am gone I need you to watch over this one. So I have appointed her as your handmaiden, to see to your needs in your coming trials."

But the Queen was very nearly seeing red.

"What? Why?" she asked, and though they spoke in private, well out of others hearing, her voice was clipped and agitated.

"I have an odd feeling about her. And I want her under close supervision," he said, still holding the Queen's hand.

"Are you *sure* that's what it's really about?" the Queen asked, accusation in her voice.

The God-King stiffened before her.

"Very well, if you chafe at this task, I shall take her with me and make sure she gets up to no mischief," he said gruffly in return.

"Oh, I am certain you would like that," the Queen bit back, "perhaps that was your plan all along."

Kulav's brow furrowed and he looked offended. Then upset.

"Fine, I'll take the wench on," the Queen said, her voice a little shrill.

"Think of how you are leaving us on our parting day," Kulav cautioned her.

"Think of it yourself," she bit back, but instantly… absolutely instantly, she frowned and regretted it. "I'm sorry, my love," she said, letting her head hang in shame. "I'll do as you ask. I'm just… I'm so bothered with the prospect of being without you for so long to come."

All of that absolute knowing of how he felt towards her, that affection they'd shared so recently was but a distant memory, clouded by her troubled mind.

Kulav studied her a moment and nodded, squeezing her hand once more.

"As am I. But come, we must part, and do so promptly," he said, leading her back down the marble stairs and out into the courtyard.

There, Kulav's squire presented and helped him don his crescent helm and flowing cloak. His scimitar was strapped to his person using his belt and scabbard, and he made for his horse with a bound.

The night-black steed, largest in the whole of the force, took its masters' heft with minimal complaint as Kulav took the reins and peered back to his wife.

"Keep the home fires burning, my wife. For when I return, I shall be weary and victorious," he declared. "Rest assured, my fires for you shall never dim," he added on, a smile evident from beneath his helm.

"Your kingdom shall await you with anticipation, Your Greatness," she said, unable to resist the smile he brought to her own face.

But the moment was brief, and there he went, turning about and leading his troops out of the courtyard and down the spiralling roadways of Ariste.

Her eyes welled with moisture again as she mounted the stairs of the palace walls, and watched her husband ride off to war. Not just for the loss of his presence, or the risk he took, but because with him went a part of her. A very significant part that she didn't know she could continue without.

CHAPTER 19

Everyone had a task and went promptly about it, but there was only so much to do.

Mirella found herself touring the city, inspecting the battlements, the construction work on the walls and the ongoing training of the soldiers. Ariste was a long way from 'back to normal', from before Kulav's conquest, but slowly the lives of the people were becoming more consistent.

War threatened that, but Mirella did her best to preserve the progress they'd made.

Standing there, watching the sisters drill in one of Ariste's parks, she found herself battling to stay in the moment.

"Are you not pleased with the training of the newest acolytes, Your Majesty?" Svella asked, standing ever at her side as she did these days.

The Queen stirred from her troubled thoughts, and cast a thin-lipped smile to her friend.

"It's just war, Svella," Mirella said with a sigh.

Her slender shoulders relaxed from their bunched up position, but only slightly. The cool breeze brushing over her pale skin, a reprieve from the increasing heat of the season. It continually blew free a lock of blonde hair, but she insistently pushed it back into place.

"War troubles you, Your Majesty?" Svella asked casually, as if it were the simplest question ever.

It threw the Queen for a moment, before she remembered: the Ka'reem were always at war.

"I guess war isn't strange for you or the Ka'reem, Svella. I forget that sometimes," Mirella said, shaking her head in disbelief at the notion before looking out at the soldiers in their garb. The acolytes in leather and mail, trained by the raven-feathered sisters of the coven.

"We did not really have a term for war as such," Svella explained calmly. "It was just… the state of being."

"How, though? Why?" the Queen asked, brow furrowed, sounding frustrating at her inability to understand.

Svella shrugged at first, but then continued.

"There were always tribal conflicts. Usually nothing of major significance, simply raids for supply, or sorties for revenge because one tribesperson insulted or harmed another," she said, her own raven hair locked in a ponytail.

"Exhausting," the Queen said.

"It could be, yes. It was only with the rise of the God-King that we had a concept for what you might call peace. But even then, peace for us was only the interlude before grander war, with greater spoils on the line."

The Queen arched a brow, trying to wrap her head around the realities of such a life as she stared out over the trees and buildings.

"How stressful it must have been, never knowing when the next raid might happen. When you or a loved one might find yourselves cut down, taken hostage, or maimed, all over some petty vendetta or a desire for more trophies or supplies," the Queen said.

"Yes, that was the worst part of it, in many ways," Svella said in agreement.

"The waiting," Mirella said.

"Mm. The battles themselves were, of course, rough, though quite often we never sought to kill rival tribes and their members; merely wound and take what we needed. Death and terrible injury were always a distinct possibility."

"But at least that was action," Mirella said.

"Exactly," Svella concurred.

"This waiting around… the lull before the storm. Ever unsure of when the battle might begin, or what it might bring," the Queen said, taking a deep breath, her chest heaving.

"Or if we have done all we can do in preparation," Svella tacked on, smiling wryly at her Queen.

Mirella looked back to her friend, seeing she had got to the root of much of what was troubling her.

"It feels like I should be doing more, Svella," she confessed with a sigh.

"You already ordered the reinforcement of the walls, which is going apace. Ordered more training drills, stockpiled all the food and supplies we could get from the steppes in time," Svella reassured.

"Yes, but that all feels so… so inadequate," the Queen said, turning her stern gaze back upon the practicing soldiers.

"We only have so much to work with though," Svella said, pointing out the obvious.

"Only so much, yes," Mirella muttered, though her mind began to whir with the possibilities. "We have but a few Aristean women who have chosen to prove themselves for service, right Svella?"

"Correct, Your Majesty," Svella said, nodding once.

"But we haven't been truly encouraging them to sign up and attempt the trials, have we?" she said more than asked, but raised her brow at her friend in questioning all the same.

"True…" Svella said, sounding a little hesitant. "But it is unlikely many Aristean women — or men for that matter — would pass our rigorous trials, Your Majesty."

"Then little will change, will it?" Mirella responded with a grin, steepling her fingers in thought. "Perhaps part of the problem is lack of incentive. You Ka'reem do it for glory, to honour your family and ancestors, because it is destiny. The people of Ariste see themselves first and foremost as commoners, doing menial tasks."

Svella rolled the idea around in her own head, slowly seeming to warm to the idea.

"What can we offer them then?"

That gave Mirella a moment for pause, but the Queen eventually came up with something.

"Full status, equal to that of any Ka'reem. A stipend, and freedom to found their own lineage, free of Aristean custom and law," she declared at last, smugly proud of herself for the idea.

"Excellent, Your Majesty. Though… only the God-King himself can grant the first point. The best you can officially offer is your endorsement to him," Svella explained.

And the Queen bristled inside.

She knew what Svella was saying was right, before she ever said it. Yet somehow she'd gone ahead and said it anyhow.

And then Mirella felt frustrated and annoyed for it.

"Yvel!" came the Queen's harshly clipped words.

"Yes, Your Majesty?" came the woman's response, as she strode up from her position well out of sight, just as the Queen preferred.

"Send word. Have the crier prepare an announcement. All citizens shall be expected to come listen to their Queen."

***

It didn't take long to arrange such a thing under normal circumstances, but with the ongoing training, the absence of the bulk of their forces, and the Queen's own insistence upon proceeding in a very formal, regal manner, delayed the announcement by a few days.

"This at least has livened up the city, made the waiting less anxious," the Queen said approvingly as she looked out over her assembled subjects in the largest plaza of Ariste.

Svella stood by her side, as ever, both bodyguard and adjutant.

"People must be kept busy during the waiting, or else they begin to suffer from doubts and rebellious thoughts," Svella stated.

"Precisely," the Queen declared, smiling proudly.

Laid out before her were thousands of Aristeans, all eagerly awaiting the word of their Queen. The clarion call went out, the horns playing the official notes of announcement for the rightful ruler. The same melody played for many long ages.

"Citizens of Ariste, your rightful ruler by blood and birth, Queen Annabelle Flair!" the crier declared, leaving off the usual tail end part about being wife of the God-King.

It was a notable absence to Svella and the other Ka'reem, and one the Queen tactically devised to win the sympathy of the crowds more effectively.

She was their rightful ruler, after all.

With a regal smile upon her face, and a crown upon her head, she stepped forward to the podium to the cheers and applause of her people. It was her first public address without the God-King since… well, since Mirella had taken possession of the body.

The crowds of native Aristeans seemed to approve of it, albeit hesitantly.

"My people," she began, her tone of voice so formal and elegant. "There have been rough times for Ariste. The long peace we enjoyed was stripped from us, our city lit aflame. But through it all, here we still stand."

The crowd cheered louder after that, losing some of their inhibitions.

"We find ourselves now at a crossroads. With so many of the Ka'reem forces away, the city's defense and well-being falls squarely upon my shoulders alone."

That line didn't get full cheers, but gazing out at the people, the Queen could see they peered at her with expectant wonder. Many dared not think of what she might be leading to with this.

"It is a great burden to bear, that puts monumental decisions before me, my people. Yet one thing remains true: you are my first responsibility. Before my own well-being and safety, I must do what is right for Ariste."

The crowds were eating out of her hand, she thought.

"I was left with a small force to defend us all, of hardened Ka'reem warriors. Yet to me, the heart of Ariste is her people. And though we may rely upon these women to keep us safe, our hearts beat furiously."

More loud cheers, cries of devotion to their Queen. She could even see some weeping at her words as she continued on.

"So, as rightful ruler of Ariste, I turn to you, my people. I ask of you something immense, to serve me, to serve Ariste… as you never have before."

She delayed a moment, letting that hang in the air expectantly as she raised a hand.

"Sign up to serve under the Raven Guard sisters. Take the trials, and give it your all. Show me your vigor, show me your dedication. Show me your fire, Ariste! Prove that you can be a match for a Ka'reem warrior, and make me proud!"

Her words caught them by surprise, but slowly applause and cheers built. Higher and higher the noise went, until at last some called her name.

She bid them silent again with her hand, smiling brightly.

"Now, I do not ask this of you unrewarded, my subjects. To train and do the trials is no easy task. To patrol our streets, keep the peace and defend our city, are monumental responsibilities. And so I offer you these things for your service…"

She wet her lips as she watched the crowd, eyes wide, awaiting her words.

"As you all know," she began, building to it slowly, "we have faced great cultural upheaval as of late, amid all the rest. The Ka'reem's ways are different than our own. They have not the formal binds of lineage, the formal duty to one's line beyond all else but service to Ariste and her Queen."

She took a pause once more, surveying the crowds that stood, rapt.

"Many of you find yourself in bondage to family Houses under distant relatives who care little for you.

Sold into arranged marriages you had no plans for. Well… should you pass the trials and serve your time with the warriors, you shall be freed of these obligations. Open to found your own lineage, by your own choosing."

That drew gasps and then thunderous applause. For though the old customs were ingrained in Aristean culture, they were despised by all but the oldest and those it benefited the most.

"Furthermore," she said, raising a hand and bringing an end to their applause, "a generous stipend shall be provided for all who serve as warriors. As well as pension upon release from duty."

The people clearly loved that, though the dour faces of the old and those who stood not to benefit peppered about.

"Finally," she stated loudly, her voice carrying down from her elevated podium, draped with fine purple velvets, "for the duration of my lone protectorship, all who serve shall have fully equal status to any Ka'reem warrior. And by the spirits…" she said, biting her lower lip, trying to suppress her urge to say what she knew she shouldn't.

The inner battle was tough, that deviousness inside… wanting her to pledge what she knew she shouldn't. To undermine the God-King and build her people's faith in her and her alone.

"When the God-King returns…" she said, trying to effect a steady, commanding countenance even as she fought internally, "I shall press the case on all your behalf, to convince him… to continue that practice forever more."

She managed to avoid promising what she shouldn't, and did not undermine Kulav, but still… it made the crowds happy.

They cheered and applauded, and some in the younger ones especially chant her name.

The Queen basked in their approval awhile, smiling out at them until at last she tried to bid them to silence once more.

"Do this for me, my people. For Ariste. For your brothers and sisters, mothers and fathers. For us all! Let Ariste have her own people back in charge of patrolling our streets, manning the walls. And more than that… prove to our new Ka'reem brethren that we are worthy and stand equal! Show your pride!"

The crowd went wild at her emotive speech, thousands crying out, even many of the older ones who had been dour and quiet before. They raised their fists and chanted her name, churning the whole city into an uproar.

CHAPTER 20

"The repairs on the city wall are going well, Your Majesty. However, the masons and stoneworkers report that one segment of the wall in the eastern section over here is under severe distress and in jeopardy of collapse if serious work is not done."

"Then it needs to be done," the Queen said imperiously.

"It is not that simple," said Inyis, the Raven Guardswoman put in charge of overseeing the civilian efforts.

"Then what is the matter?"

"The repairs would take a full year, realistically, Your Majesty," Inyis stated.

"How could the walls have been allowed to fall into such a state at all without anyone noticing?" the Queen asked, sounding disturbed.

"That's the issue, Your Majesty. The wall itself there is fine, it is the earth beneath it."

"I don't understand, Inyis," the Queen said.

"They tell me that the mountain's underwater stream runs down along there, and has been wearing away the foundation for some time. It shall be a heavy undertaking to dig down, divert the water and reinforce the foundation. I think a year is being optimistic on that front, but the builders did not seem to wish to provide a longer time frame and risk displeasing you," Inyis said.

The Queen furrowed her brow and thought on this a while.

"How long would it take to simply divert the water flow itself? Because if we postpone the repairs and leave it at that, the walls will show no weakness and it should last us through the battle, at the very least, should it not?"

Inyis thought on this a moment, the short woman chosen for her position because of her lack of physical power as much as her aptitude with such clerical and bureaucratic matters as organizing reconstruction.

"I shall consult the workers, but that might just be doable, Your Majesty," Inyis said, bowing her head.

"Your Majesty," said the guard at the entrance to the throne room, "the Imperial Ambassador is here to seek your audience."

Mirella arched a brow curiously from her work.

The Queen had been studying a map of the city with Svella and some of her advisors, planning for the battles to come. The last thing she expected was a visit from the almost-forgotten ambassador.

"And what is his purpose?" she asked, sounding confused.

"He wishes to discuss terms for reparations," stated the guard in her raven garb.

The Queen rolled her eyes and looked to Svella, the two bemused by the idea.

"Well… what a lovely waste of time that is. Keep him waiting out there, while I decide what to do with him," she said, returning her gaze to the map in her lap.

That was when Yvel decided to speak up, cast to the corner as an unused handmaid to the Queen. She'd been consulted so rarely that Yvel wouldn't even know if the Queen was pregnant or not.

"Excuse me, Your Majesty," Yvel said, hands clasped behind her back beneath her cloak.

The Queen grit her teeth at the very sound of the woman's voice, giving a look to Svella that said it all.

Another annoying interruption.

"What is it?" she asked in a clipped voice, her slender fingers clutching her magnifying glass uncomfortably tight.

"Perhaps I might go and tend to—"

The Queen cut her off.

"Yes, that sounds excellent. Go do that," she said, immediately turning her attention back to the other women at her sides. "So then, about the eastern wall…"

Yvel bowed, then said not a word before slipping out the rear door.

It took her awhile to round the building and come to the waiting chambers. Though thankfully, the servant's entrance let her slip in without alerting the guards outside the room.

There, Adom waited, sat down upon a seat holding a scroll and ledger, looking rather surprised to see her.

He was wise enough not to say anything incriminating, though.

"What are you doing here?" Yvel said, a little impatiently.

"I am here to present a proposal to the Queen, hopefully to play upon her sympathies for the Empire, seeing as she was always an advocate of ours. What with the new moves she's made, I thought it would be a good time—"

He was cut off by Yvel.

"Are you a fool? The Queen is not on your side. Not at all," Yvel said, eyes wide.

"Well... "Adom said, rubbing a hand back over his hair, "at the very least I thought I might buy some time with more bartering."

Yvel shook her head impatiently.

"You merely reminded her of your existence. Made it more likely that she will off you now. You are playing a dangerous game," she said.

"If I didn't know better, I would swear you sound concerned," he said, brow raised, studying the change in her demeanor curiously. It wasn't a smug declaration, he was genuinely surprised, and curious.

Yvel clenched her fists and stared down at the man.

"You had best hide, if you wish to keep living. And being of use to me," she said.

"Hide where?" he asked.

"Come find me when you smarten up. If it's not already too late, that is," she said, before vanishing through the servant's door once more.

CHAPTER 21

"Ambassador Adom Frenel," announced the guard, rather unceremoniously, leaving off his titles, even the Empire to which he served. An obvious slight.

He strode on through anyhow, finding himself meeting before the Queen; and her alone.

That gave him hope.

Hope that the Queen wished to talk serious business with him, out of the prying ears of the savage guardians she was appointed. Hope that he might appeal to her roots.

"Your Ma—" he was cut off by the guard.

"Her Majesty, Queen Annabelle Flair of Ariste and the Flower Fields," came her introduction, after which Adom was compelled to give another bow.

"Your Majesty, it is an honour," he began again as the doors were pulled shut behind him, leaving them alone together.

"Ambassador Frenel," came her response, sitting there regally atop the throne, her pink lips spread into a smile. "At last we speak again."

"Indeed, Your Majesty," he said, smiling himself in return. "It has been long overdue."

"And finally we may speak more frankly, Ambassador," she said, looking so regal upon the massive throne, even if it was of Ka'reem make.

"How relieving that is to hear, Your Majesty. I have ever trusted that you were the utmost voice of reason in Ariste, and I can still remember your letters and visit when you were but a girl," he said, attempting to play upon sympathies.

Truth of the matter was that he was there for her youthful visit to the Imperial seat, but paid her little to no heed at the time. She was just one princeling among many.

"It is good to know that my well-being has meant so much to the Empire, after the initial attempts to come rescue me and Ariste went so… awry," she said, her arms upon the rests of the throne, back straight.

"Indeed it has, Your Majesty. And the death of your fiancé, which would have ushered in a period of closer relations between the Empire and Ariste, was a tragic blow. Despite all that has happened, and all you have been forced to do… it pleases us to see you strong and resilient upon the throne."

She gave a tight-lipped smile to that, her elegant sky-blue gown edged with frills at her sleeves, high collar and train.

"I am making the most of what cards I have been dealt, Ambassador. You of all people understand that, no?" she said, arching a singular brow.

"Absolutely, Your Majesty. I have heard of your new measures, to get native Aristeans back into command of their own destiny. Surely before long you will have plenty of your loyal subjects back into positions of guardianship."

"Enough of my own loyal subjects to govern and protect my city once more," she said, rather boldly.

Boldly enough to make Adom pause.

"Your Majesty is most wise and daring," he said, bowing to her once more.

"Wise and daring, perhaps. But I have limited resources. Time is of the essence, and while I have willing bodies signing up to defend my city, they are lacking in training, and reliant upon the Raven guard for that and arms," she said, strumming her long nails upon the throne.

"Of course, Your Majesty. That is a dire situation to be in. Most dire indeed. And while the King is away..." he trailed, playing coy.

"If only I had some way to get aid, support, or even messages out, without having to rely upon the Ka'reem... how much better things could be for us here, Ambassador," she said smoothly. Pointedly.

"Indeed, Your Majesty. I would love to be able to help," he said.

"And can you, Ambassador?" she asked, staring down at him with an intense gaze.

Silence permeated the air between them in the lonely throne room.

"Not in my current capacity, Your Majesty. However… I shall endeavour to look into it for you, if it pleases you. I wish to be of all the aid that I might be. For all you have done for the Empire, for all you mean to it, I shall not rest until your throne is safe."

"Thank you, Ambassador. I shall look forward to our next conversation," she said, smiling pleasantly as he bowed before her.

"I shall seek you out immediately, once I have something to report. Sooner rather than later, I hope," he said, backing away towards the doors.

"Excellent," was her final response.

CHAPTER 22

Adom Frenel headed through the courtyard of the palace, skirting the throngs of Aristeans that were undergoing training through the Queen's new initiative.

All around, tall, stern-looking women of the Raven Guard inspected the struggling hopefuls and barked orders at them, drilling them in the rigours of Ka'reem military lifestyle.

His two guards, the 'escorts' that accompanied him everywhere, stopped, and the lead one looked to him.

"The Queen has said you're clear to walk freely now. If you desire our escort, that is purely up to you."

Adom hesitated, looked into the eyes of the guards that had been hounding him closely for weeks.

"Ah, very well. Thank you," he said with a smile. "The Queen is most wise. You two can wait at my residence, I'm going to tour the grounds a bit before heading back. I'll be safe here."

"Very well," came the gruff response before they headed off.

Adom was true to his word, slowly taking his time, touring about the palace grounds, studying the trainees.

Though truthfully, his purpose was something else altogether.

He sought signs of someone tailing him, peering about everywhere as inconspicuously as he could.

Nothing stood out to him, but he carried on, hands behind his back as he made his way out of the courtyard and into the streets of Ariste itself.

The streets were bustling with life, for though the city was preparing for war the citizenry were busy preparing their own means while continuing on with their daily affairs as best as possible.

Slowly winding his way on down the hillside city, he stopped occasionally at market booths, or crafts-people's tables, inspecting items and looking like a casual tourist.

It took him about an hour of meandering through the streets before he started to notice the telltale signals of a professional following him.

She was good, whoever she was. She looked like any other citizen at first, then a while later donned a cloak and hood. Then the hood was gone when next he caught glimpse of her.

Then her hair was tied back.

All told, he spent about two hours confirming his suspicions.

The Queen was having him followed, but wished him to think he wasn't. That she was on his side. And that meant she intended him to lead her to something secret.

Adom was only newly ambassador, but he grew up in the Imperial courts. He understood such machinations, and wasn't about to be fooled by them.

The Queen had her own plots, but whatever they were, they didn't involve any loyalty to the Empire. If she wished to undermine the God-King, as she so indicated to him in their private meeting, she wished to do so for her own purposes.

Most importantly, it meant he could trust a certain someone else more.

Or at least, he hoped so.

He wasted as little time after that as he could manage without raising suspicion.

Taking twists and turns, weaving through the thickest crowd he could find, he made his way towards his residence before sidestepping down an alley.

Yvel had not given him much to go on to find her, but he knew how to get in touch with her.

He moved on down the dimly lit alleyway, then took a right. A left. Came to a small little garden around a seldom used well.

There, he pulled up a bucket from the well, and the reason for why it was so little used became apparent.

It was a strain to pull the heavy weight, and once it was up, the bucket was clearly only half-full of water. The rest of the weight was some quartz-like stone from within the well.

Rooting through the bucket, Adom took two shimmering wet stones and placed them upon the rim of the well before letting the bucket plunge back down underwater.

With that, he had nothing more to do but move on. And wait.

CHAPTER 23

"How progresses the new recruits' training?" the Queen asked of Svella and her advisors.

"Well, all things considered," Svella said, heading off the other women around the oval table.

"They are doing better than many of us expected, but still, a number of them are not all they could be," added Inyis, with nods from some of the others.

"The Aristeans need pre-training before taking their trials," the Queen declared, knitting her fingers together as she peered down the table.

"Pre-training, Your Majesty?" asked one of the women.

"Yes. You Ka'reem spend your whole lives being prepared for the rigours of the trials, but Aristeans lead different lives. Most of them only ever spend time preparing to become blacksmiths, stable hands, or maids. A brief introductory training session into combat, to get their physical fitness up, should improve the numbers we get dramatically," she said.

The proposal got some dubious looks, but Svella was smiling at the idea.

"An excellent proposal, Your Majesty. It might help level the playing field some. Although..." she looked at the other women a moment, "I expect the other warrior-concubines shall have issue suppressing their snickers at having to teach people in rudimentary fighting like they were children."

That got laughs from around the table, from all except the Queen herself.

"Well," the Queen said, licking her lips, "we shall have to do our best to balance our urge to laugh with our necessity to see more capable soldiers in defense of our city."

One of the older women leaned forward.

"Do we not worry that this coddling will lead to a dilution of the forces' strength, Your Majesty?"

Mirella narrowed her eyes at that question, staring down the table at the lady.

"An advantage over another bestowed by fate or circumstance does not make one inherently superior. To have the advantage of prior training is something easily rectified and in no way a dilution of skill. Unless, of course, you are afraid that the Aristeans might surprise you with their competency after such trainings, hmm?"

Mirella crossed her arms over her chest and let the challenge hang there. Everyone knew better than to speak up.

Everyone except Yvel, off standing in the corner.

"Does that mean that any woman might have been in your shoes were but fickle fate more fortunate upon their birthing, Your Majesty?" she asked, in an obvious challenge to her words.

The Queen bristled, but Mirella was quick to answer anyhow.

"Perhaps so, Yvel. But we shall never know on that particular count, shall we?" Mirella said smoothly.

The topics of the meeting addressed, the women all rose shortly after Mirella herself. The stately woman's slender form betrayed the slight bump of a burgeoning child within her womb.

"Thank you all for your analysis. Svella, a word. And Yvel," she said, not looking to the woman, "tend to some of these trainings yourself. I am interested to see how my Aristeans manage under your tutelage."

All obeyed her, of course, and within moments it was just Svella and her.

"It has been almost two months since the God-King has left, my friend… and I am anxious. So anxious," Mirella said, rubbing her forehead.

"The battle will be upon us before you know it, Mirella," Svella said, smiling down at her friend's belly. "He has gifted you with another child before departing, at least. Your life does not want for purpose as we wait."

The Queen laughed a bit dryly on that point, but nodded.

"My life has too much purpose in it, Svella, but not near enough power to see it all served," the Queen said.

"Careful, Your Majesty, the desire for power is a drug," Svella cautioned with a humorous smile.

Though Mirella's sharp glance was anything but as contemplation sank in.

CHAPTER 24

The struggle to hold onto herself was so very real to Mirella.

As pressures mounted in her attempts to rule Ariste in the God-King's absence, she felt the line between herself and who she was grow all the more tenuous. So long had passed since she swapped bodies with the erstwhile Princess, yet she still hadn't grown comfortable in her new form.

Laying there atop her opulent bed, surrounded by luxury that was hers, the drastic change in her life from servant—no, property—to Anabelle, was so stark. She lay upon smooth silk sheets that caressed her alabaster skin. A far cry from the coarse, cheap linens that were her old fare.

It was decadent living, and every silken caress of her sheets was a delight on her skin that made it easier to forget who she was.

No, she thought, cradling her growing belly. *I must hold on*, and she had to. She couldn't let go of who she was without losing it all.

She sweat, even though it was no longer warm. Her gossamer gown did little to hide her curvaceous form. The swell of her breasts, the round of her tummy.

Mirella forced her mind to focus on Kulav. Her God-King. Her anchor.

He, more than anything else, more than any man, reminded her of who she really was.

From the moment she had laid eyes upon his towering, obsidian frame, she was captivated.

For years, she had not felt like a woman, never like a person. Always someone's property, someone's object of desire at best. That left her uninterested in men or romance for almost her entire life.

Then…

There he was.

He was broad. He was tall. He was everything a man should be.

Handsome, strong, confident. Powerful.

A master of his own destiny.

And some part of her could sense upon first meeting that glorious warlord that his life was not like that of other powerful men. He did not have his right to rule handed to him. He claimed it through a life of hardship.

He was everything she could have ever dreamed of and more.

Picturing him upon that first meeting, illuminated by the fires of Ariste, solidified his love in her consciousness. Kept her solid, even as it stirred her loins and made her feel hot and moistened.

Her eyes were shut as she pictured him, and her hands began to move without her so much as thinking on it.

She was a ruler now, in a different body, but her flesh kindled in response to him nonetheless.

Her fingers slipped down beneath her gauzy panties, finding her labia puffy and slick.

Mirella had pleasured herself many times in the past throughout her lonely, desperate life. But never did she find herself so aroused through it. She hadn't met the man who would explode her expectations, who would set the new bar for her desires.

And where sliding her dainty fingers along that pussy slit of hers, teasing her clit, was just a way to pass time, to distract herself from her loneliness, her misery… it had instead become a way of reminding her of all she had. All she'd accomplished.

All she was and wanted.

She whimpered in thought, desperately missing her husband and ruler. Wishing for all the world that he would be back in her arms, in her bed.

Her mind reached out across the plains as her fingers squelched in her loins, her other hand reaching up to cup at her engorged breast, to squeeze the milk-laden tit and simulate as best she could His touch.

Though as she pictured him over her, his thick, rippling abs and pecs on display, his throbbing manhood held in hand ready to spear her... she felt something so intense.

It wasn't climax—it was sweeter still.

It was his presence. Not imagined, not a figment of desire, but his presence. True and genuine.

When she flung open her eyelids, she saw him.

Though he wasn't over her. Instead, he lay there in his tent, and she knew she was no longer in her bedroom. Her consciousness had drifted across great distances to be with him, and she knew it to be fact despite how little sense it made to her.

There he was, the God-King Kulav, laying upon a simple mat on the ground, with no company but a bottle at his side.

His eyes were shut as he lay there slumbering, but Mirella missed him so dearly.

She slipped to her knees beside him and very nearly wept upon the spot.

Her love, her King. Her husband.

Desire, need, and whatever powers that had been awakened in her in recent years had brought her to his side, and she could not help but reach out to touch him. To ensure she was not delusional.

Though the moment she touched his hard, dark flesh, she knew it was impossible to fake.

And his reaction too real.

Her pale digits roamed along the grooves of his bulging muscles, on down from his pecs, and he stirred gently. His broad frame restlessly shifting, a low, husky groan rumbling from his chest.

He knew her touch, even in his slumber. Even from across space itself.

She continued to let her fingers trail down to the rim of his waist, feeling the indents in his sculpted body as she gently began to work his belt open. Her own loins burned with such need, but upon seeing her husband again, she was overtaken with purpose.

To serve him as she'd not been able to since he left.

Mirella freed his manhood from his leather trousers, that obsidian pillar rising up immediately. Her touch had awoken his desires even in his sleep, and she gazed longingly at the bulging, veiny girth that had given her more pleasure and purpose than anything else.

She worshipped her husband, and more to the point: she worshipped that part of him.

Kneeling beside him, she bent over, let his fragrant musk fill her nose, causing her nostrils to flare.

It was all so beautifully real, so perfect. And she savoured him as she leaned down, licked along the underside of his cock, starting from his heavy balls on up to the very tip of his pulsating manhood.

That elicited a deep, rumbling moan from him, and his eyes opened if only for a moment.

"Mirella…" he let out in a husky mutter.

It pleased her so to hear that, to know that she was the first he thought of in his desires. Or even that her techniques were so unique that they immediately brought her — the pleasure she brought — to his mind.

He reached out, his bulging arm lifting up as his immense palm rested upon her head. He stroked her hair, caressed her blonde tresses as he moaned with each lick of her tongue.

Just as she felt his presence so intimately, he too had to feel the same, and she bent down further, swirling her tongue around his balls, lavishing those thick, cum-laden testicles of his with such devotion.

No part of his loins would miss out on her efforts, her worshipful lashings and slow, suckling of his balls making them both moan with delight.

"Mirella," he said again, his cock disgorging some of his salty precum as she worked his balls so intimately and wrapped her dainty fingers about the base of his shaft, slowly pumping his length.

Her breasts grazed his thigh as she began to slide her tongue up his length once more, kissing at his cock as she worked her hand along his immense bulk as best she could with her tiny grasp.

When she came to the crown of His Majesty's magnificent organ, she kissed and licked, tasting his flavourful gift before gently tugging back his skin and intimately making out with the fullness of that purple, flared tip.

Her every motion was slow and meticulous, no rushing. No hurrying on towards the finish. She was enjoying him, and he was enjoying her. The two of them surrendering to slow bliss, admiring the beauty of each other's bodies.

For as she laved his dick with her warm, wet tongue and pouty lips, he grew more animated. Awakened.

He rubbed his hand down her spine, felt her rear and squeezed her flesh. Her thin, gauzy nightgown so skimpy and flimsy, doing little to inhibit his fondling and roaming hands as the second one came to squeeze at her dangling breasts.

Mirella whimpered and moaned, arching her spine, pushing her tits down into his palm as she licked and suckled upon his cock. She was so attentive though, never losing focus on her true mission: to pay homage to his dark glory, to his spectacular manhood, the temple of his body.

Kulav's powerful hips rocked in time with her motions, even as she tried to urge him to stillness with her tender touches. She wanted to bring him to completion slowly, in her own time and manner.

She could feel his cock pulsate betwixt her two pouty lips, not the fast, urgent pulse of a quick and hard-earned climax, but a slow, thick throb of a steadily building pleasure.

He groaned aloud, and she could taste his seed upon her tongue, the precum flowing thicker as his balls began to tighten with his impending release.

"Fuck, Mirella," he growled out.

She didn't know what magic had allowed her to feel him once more, but to taste his cock seemed as real as it could be. Her body moved in tandem with his, enjoying the pulsing of his veins against her exploratory tongue.

That was who she was. She was powerful, but she would always willingly submit to him, her husband and her God.

In that moment of peace and clarity, she felt her old consciousness, her gratitude, begin to flood her awareness. It soothed away the devious thoughts that plagued her to seize more.

She tightened her lips, swirling her tongue and working his cock incessantly, pulling him towards his satisfying end with her mouth.

Her fingers dipped beneath, finding his heavy sac, those dainty alabaster fingers massaging him. She pulled them down, prolonging and intensifying his own pleasure, and he growled again, awake and yet content to allow her to work.

How often had she paid reverence to his body in such a way? Thrown herself to his mercy, forgotten about her own yearnings and pleasure for she found it within pleasing him?

She shuddered at the white-hot thought, at the memories of how suckling him gave her greater purpose in life.

The tip of her tongue ran along the flared crown of his head, over his frenum, moaning as his breathing stalled.

With a loud gasp and a shudder, he found his satisfaction, that thick, hard dick of his swelling almost beyond the point she could stretch her jaw. Then the creamy hot spurts of his seed began to jet, so much white spunk coating her tongue and tonsils, firing down her throat.

He had so much to give, and she claimed it all upon her knees.

Spurt after spurt of that thick cum filled her mouth until she had no choice but to swallow it down and make room for the oncoming gushes.

They continued together like that, until he was spent for the moment and breathing heavily. His ebon torso glistening in the dim candlelight of the tent, showing off his muscles.

His eyes opened, blinking as he pushed himself to his elbows and found himself gazing at his wife in quiet wonder.

"How…?" he began, reaching out once more, stroking her hair, touching her shoulder, marvelling at the fact he could not only see but also feel her. "My love…" he muttered in disbelief, so smitten at the sight of her.

It was how pleased he was to see her that made her own pulsing need between her thighs so much more intense.

To know that she lusted for him and loved him was what brought her back to feeling like herself, but to see how much he adored her made her heart swim. She licked her lips free of his marks, her tender mouth tingling with sensation as she moved up his body.

She could smell him, taste him, feel him. His body and presence took over her mind, her heart thudding so quickly in her chest.

"I needed to see you," she murmured before her lips found his, her little tongue prodding his much larger mouth. She was ravenous for him, needed to feel his passion.

Kulav was never meek enough of a man to shy away from kissing her after such an act. He was big, he was strong, he was dauntless.

So together their tongues slashed and danced, their lips smacking and pressing together, and all the while, she could feel his hard dick throb against her belly, losing none of its potent stiffness.

Those strong hands of his travelled up and down her sides, felt her hips, explored her body. Partly, it seemed to be about seeing if she was real, not some figment of his imagination, or worse. But much more it was just about savouring the touch of his wife after so long apart.

When at last their lips broke apart long enough for words to slip free, albeit brief as that was, he spoke in a husky voice.

"How is it possible? The city? You didn't leave it without you…" he said, and already she could feel that he was understanding what was going on.

Understanding as well as he could, anyway. As either of them could. The powers of the witches were far from knowable craftwork, but forever a mystery even to its practitioners.

"I closed my eyes in Ariste and I opened them here to find you," Mirella whispered. Her lips moved to his broad throat, her tongue running along it, tasting the bit of saltiness on his skin. "I've missed you so."

Without him, she had been losing herself, as if the ground had been sundered beneath her. But then, back with him, her body pressed against his, her foundation grew hard once more.

With his answer provided, he dove back into kissing her, hard and deep. His hand went to the back of her head, knitting his fingers through her hair as he grasped her hip and rear with his other hand.

As his cock pulsed beneath her, still slick from her saliva after the cleaning she gave him, he swiftly twisted about, placing her onto her back, beneath him.

"My love... even in my dreams you were with me. But even if that is all this is, a dream... it is sweet release from the torture of your absence," he said, gentle and careful of her pregnant belly as he kissed and fondled her with passionate fire.

She hadn't needed to tell him of her pregnancy. It was as known to both of them that last day together, in their own way. They knew she would swell with his child as clearly as they knew the sun would rise at dawn.

Her form writhed against his, her little moans peppered against his tongue.

He spoke in between kisses, his hands undoing her nightgown, freeing her breasts to his hard, groping grasp.

"This whole excursion makes me doubt myself more than anything," he said, lunging for her mouth once more. "The need to conquer pales in comparison to my need to take you. It lives in the shadow of my need to rut you into the dirt and breed you to the end of our days, my wife."

His hand grew too bold and squeezed her breast enough to make her whimper and squeak, but then the feel of his cock prodding at her cunny, nudging at her slick little slit covered only by that sheer pair of panties.

She spread her legs eagerly, shifting down just so that he'd press against her all the more.

They'd changed each other so much, found such joy and desire in one another. She had to hold onto that, to those sweet words he rewarded her with. The risks he'd taken to have her as his own were monumental, after all. He'd sacrificed so much to be hers, given in to so many of her demands and whims.

Because he truly, earnestly loved her in return.

Yet as he tugged her panties aside and pushed up, that thick beast of a cock sank into her honeyed loins, it was easy to feel who was in charge. To feel that his command was real, physical.

Primal.

He gave a deep, lewd groan as that immense member spread her open wide, splaying her cunny lips about his shaft. Every pulse of his desire was felt through her being as he squeezed her breast and looked down upon her with such wanton lust.

"Kulav," she moaned upon her wispy voice, her body pinned beneath him as her legs wrapped around his waist. Her hands found his shoulders as his mouth crashed against hers once more, bruising her with the intensity as he nestled within her body.

"Mirella," came his own husky voice in return.

Together they were united again, and though she had only just brought him to climax, he was rock-solid and filled with passion for her.

Pumping his hips, he began to fuck her right there on the ground, his heavy balls swaying as he plunged in deep, only to tug back against the pull of her cunny lips.

She could see the strain of pleasure on his face, the sound of desire on his breath, the look of love in his eyes.

He leaned in, kissed her again, again, bit her lower lip hungrily. He was ravenous for her after so long apart.

"I should have collared and chained you and never let you leave my side," he declared in his lust-filled daze. "You are mine and should forever be kept with me."

A shiver of pleasure went through her, primal and dark. She was surprised by how those words affected her after all she'd been through, how much they aroused her. She'd escaped slavery through her love of him, and so readily would go back to chains if it meant never being apart from him.

She moaned as her back arched, her nipples stiffening against his chest as the thought toyed within her.

Their bodies made such sweet asymmetry. Hers shapely and pale with soft curves, his dark and mighty, with hard bulges and ridges.

As he rose back up, arching his spine as he thrust his cock into her, she wanted so desperately to still kiss him and went for his forearm beside her head. She kissed at the bulging veins there, which ran along his thick arm.

"My sweet pet," he growled, his cock swelling inside her with his rising pace, crashing his loins into hers as he gave her breast a squeeze.

She'd been so long without him that his body felt larger than ever, the sweet reprieve of his absence filling her with almost a drugged high. Everything felt so intense, from the way his hand gripped her tender breast to the beats of his heart felt through their primal connection.

"I would gladly be collared to you," she whimpered out, and even she was surprised at the lust-filled words, the truth undeniably lingered behind them.

The God-King lunged for her lips again, his leather trousers down from his ass as he pounded into her harder, faster. He was driven wild with his lusts, the same warlord who had years ago stolen her breath away. Then her heart.

He reached his hand in along her thigh, right in between them. His thumb rubbed and circled at her clit as he bucked wildly.

Sparks began between her thighs, jolting through her body, making her whimper and moan with such need as he kept up the diligent work. He knew just how to tease her body, to bend it to pleasures she'd never experienced before him.

She sucked in breath as that warmth spread from her belly out, her skin feeling so much warmer than it had mere seconds ago.

While all through those intensifying feelings, her stunningly gorgeous man pounded into her, hammering his strong hips down, filling her with his hard cock as their lips tore at one another's.

His lips broke from hers with a smack, kissing along her jaw to her ear, then on down to her sensitive, slender neck. There, he bit at her skin, teased and tortured her with his ravenous hunger, pounding harder as he grunted and groaned.

"Cum for me," he commanded. "Cum on my cock and sing my praises to the stars!"

She tensed at his words, a tightness forming throughout all her muscles. And then, like a coil springing free, the tension released. Her body trembled against his as explosive pleasure touched her all over, from her toes to the tip of her head, filling her to the brim with bliss.

And she screamed. Whether it was obedience or just an urge that wouldn't be denied, she screamed his name for any to hear.

He pummeled her pussy through the whole of her climax, thrusting in even as her juices gushed out. The wet squelch of her cunny, the moist smack of his heavy balls stroking her wet ass, all filling the air as he roared in triumph at pleasing his wife.

His knees were parted, planted onto the mat as he pressed into her deeply, the whole of his gorgeous physique on display as he sank his shaft in and felt his own release so close. Each new rutting thrust into her wet cunt making his muscular body twitch with delight.

The sensations were slow to ebb, but they eventually did, and her breathing slowed to normal, a newfound warmth lingering in her heart. The loneliness had been shooed away, and in its place, love had taken a firmer hold upon her.

Kulav kept pounding into her, making her breasts jiggle and her body rock, but he forced open his eyes to tiny slits to gaze down at her.

His full lips parted with his moans, and she could see the tension run up through his muscles, his pecs twitching, his veins bulging across his hulking physique.

The God-King moaned, panted and then shuddered, never missing a beat of his hammering cock as he finally exploded into her.

More thick gouts of his cum filled her already-seeded insides until he pulled back, and the last few strands of his spunk splattered upon her pussy and panties, leaving her soiled and coated in his virility.

His chest heaved, and he looked down at her, resting upon his haunches.

"If this is but a dream, I do not wish to awaken. And if it is real, I hope it never ends," he said, looking down over her with such love and devotion in his gaze.

His weight pressed down on her, holding her still. His heart still raced and she could feel it, their beats synchronizing. It bound them together, and her arms wrapped around his chest.

"I feel like I've only been half of myself without you, my King," she murmured, finding his ear and planting a gentle kiss against it.

He lowered himself down, curling beside her, pressing her into his body.

"And I have been at best a man with purpose, but no passion," he said, kissing her forehead and hair. "Can this moment last?" he asked, though she had no answers for him. No knowing if it would last, or even if she could ever replicate it.

If it was something born of a desperate need not to lose herself to the madness that haunted and tormented her. The parts of herself that were so unlike herself.

She licked her lips, allowing his warm body to encompass hers, their breathing calm, deep, and relaxed.

"If only I knew," she murmured, and already, sleep was threatening her. "I would love to wake in your arms, to feel your stiffness and send you off fulfilled."

He kissed her, stroked her hair and held her tightly.

"Stay with me as long as you can, my love, promise me that. It's all I ask," he murmured.

And promise she did.

"I swear, my love. I am empty without you."

Kulav held her close for hours into the night, the talk between them carrying on as if they had never parted.

"I have bedded a legion of women, Mirella. But none now stir my loins as you do. None have ever compared. And now no other shall ever have even a piece of my heart," he husked with a final kiss.

The two lingered together as long as magical powers beyond their comprehension allowed, on into the early morning. Though sleep eventually replaced consciousness, and when they awoke to the urgent summons of their servants…

It was apart.

Mirella awoke to a sticky mess atop her opulent bed, surrounded by the trappings of a life she wasn't born into. Absent of her lover, who kept her both grounded and fulfilled.

CHAPTER 25

It was the middle of the day, a time when it normally would have been quite hard for Yvel to slip away for a secret rendezvous with the closely-watched Adom. However, with her new station as handmaiden to the Queen, she found herself with a great deal of free time, and less supervision than ever.

He was walking through the streets along the market when he saw her down the end of an alleyway. She promptly disappeared but he followed after her.

Again, once he reached the end, he saw her at the end of another turn, and went after her.

It happened like that for a while, with her leading him on down a path away from prying ears and eyes. For while she was not followed, he still had eyes and ears secretly upon him.

"Did they keep up?" she asked, startlingly close to him as he rounded a corner in a deep, dark back alley, shielded from the midday sun.

Adom was taken by surprise by her closeness and sudden approach after so long of a distant chase, but he quickly soothed.

He was certain he could trust her now. Or at least, certain she was the one in the city he could trust most. Whatever that meant.

"No. They keep a distant tail on me, they lose me quickly when I take diversions like this. Though they'll be suspicious for a while after," he explained, reflecting on his experience over the preceding weeks under the Queen's distant but watchful eyes.

"Then I shall be careful not to pay you another visit for some time after this," she said, crooking her lips into a wry smile.

Adom couldn't help but find himself growing fonder of the woman.

She was beautiful, sly, and oh so tempting. But more than anything, proving for himself that she was someone he could trust had let him see more fully for who she was, beyond her use to him.

It removed the anxiety that blocked him from letting his male desires run completely loose.

"You shan't have many more opportunities as is," he explained softly, running a hand back over his dark hair.

She crooked a singular brow at him in quiet questioning, cocking one elbow to the side, which had the added benefit of exposing more of her scantily clad form beneath her cloak.

Adom wanted to tell her more, but he knew he shouldn't; he was trained not to give up more than he needed. Instead, he tried to divert for a moment.

"Your letter had quite the impact," he said.

"You read it?" she asked curiously.

"Of course," he added with silent amusement. "The nature of the delivery system requires it. But nonetheless, as dubious as I was at first, I relayed the message to the Empire, along with my recommendations on the trustworthiness of the source."

"And?" she asked, oh so curious for more.

"They delivered it as you wished. And well… let's say, that all of my doubts are now vanished," he said, smiling at her pleasantly. And thought it wasn't quite true, and he still had some lingering doubts — would always have lingering doubts, about everyone and everything other than himself — he came as close to that as Adom ever possibly could.

"I hope they act upon it all," Yvel said, not allowing herself a smug smile, but a slow, hopeful nod instead.

"We shall see. I know they are intrigued with that notion. But things are already moving so fast, I don't know how it could help," he said, accidentally spilling more information than he meant to.

And for her part, Yvel picked up on it entirely.

"That soon?" she said, eyes widening.

Adom nodded slowly, too late to backpedal.

"It is unlikely we shall have another opportunity to speak again before the end," he said, a bit sad at that thought.

"Why are you still walking about freely, then?" she asked, looking him over in astonishment.

"I shall stick it out in the city to the end. It is customary for ambassadors to be held during war time. I will likely be in little danger," he said.

"You're a fool if you sincerely think that," she said, looking so very disappointed in him as she shook her head. "A damn fool, far more than I thought you capable of."

"I know your people are cruel, but the Queen is in charge here, regardless of her nature, and the battle will be over before long, I assure yo—"

"Idiot. Damnable fool," she spit. "If they are set to arrive soon, you had best make your way out. Now," she scolded, as if a harsh taskmistress talking to her pupil.

Taking a deep breath, Adom took her abuse in silence, waiting awhile before he dared speak again.

"There is no way out for me, Yvel," he said in a soft, cautious voice. "I either stay and hold out until the attack happens. Or I risk trying to escape before then. And as you know, they will undoubtedly catch me, interrogate me… and inevitably wring the truth from me. My cowardice would cost the Empire lives and I would die a coward or be shipped back home a traitor."

His declaration seemed to hit her where she didn't expect, because Yvel licked her lips and gazed down at the ground to the side.

"There is no way around it, Yvel," he said, reaching out to touch her arm sympathetically. But she immediately shrugged it off and gave him a hard look.

"You are coming with me, then," she declared gruffly.

"What?" he said, sounding confused.

"I will take you to a hideaway used by my coven," she said obstinately, chin stuck in the air.

"But I just told you, Yvel. If I go soon, it might alarm them anyh—" she cut him off again.

"They expect you to run at any moment. It will matter very little how soon or late the following attack comes," she said. And as he made to argue further, she pushed out one arm from beneath her cloak, freeing up enough of herself for him to see her flesh beneath.

Her pale stomach was swollen, clearly pregnant. And his eyes widened.

"Is… is that—" She cut him off again.

"It's mine," she said sternly. "But you and I sowed the seed of this life together. Alone," she declared. "Of that I am absolutely certain."

Adom's breath was taken away.

The news that he was fathering a child with the wild northern women had absolutely shocked him.

He gazed from her belly to her stern face a few times before shaking off his dumbfounded expression.

"What of the God-King? Didn't he—"

"No," she said curtly, cutting him off. "I did not let him touch me before he left. Though the Queen thinks it his and hates me for it all the more," she added, bending the truth about the circumstances just a little.

"But when he comes back—"

"He won't. I shall see to that," she said bitterly, eyes narrowed. "Now come with me, Adom. I have a plan to aid your army in taking the city. And you can help."

Adom was still shaken by the revelation, but he nodded, finding himself unable to muster any resistance anymore in the face of it all.

"Can I arrange to pick up some of my—"

"No. If you have anything of specifically enormous value, I shall see to it that it's gotten for you. But you must come with me now. Any further delays will only cost you your life, ultimately."

He went to speak but wasn't given the chance.

"As you said yourself. I will not be able to meet with you before the attack. Time is running short, and they will be watching you closer after this. So come, Adom," she said, much of her terse, commanding tone melting away as she cradled her belly and began to walk away. "I shall keep you safe."

CHAPTER 26

"The tedium," Mirella muttered to herself as she sat upon her throne. Alone. Svella had been assigned duties to attend to the affairs of the training, to make sure the other Raven Guard instructors were giving the Aristean volunteers a fair shake.

She strummed her fingers upon the hideously imposing throne that was Kulav's as she sat there, her mind wandering off…

Waiting gave her so much time to worry and fret. To let the darker force within her struggle against her without distraction.

She could feel it… that presence. The more time she had to combat it in silence, the more she had time to analyze it. And it scared her. The nature of her new existence, occupying a body that was not hers by birth… the sorcery that the witches had wrought for her was powerful. But it had a cost.

It always had a cost, she was warned.

The malevolence within her that sought to rose up forced her to struggle, each and every day. Struggle just to be herself. Just to maintain her control over her actions. Just to hold onto what she'd fought so hard for.

A life of consequence. A life of her own choosing.

A free woman's life.

Hers to live, give or take, if she so chose, free of the whims of an owner who bought her from someone else.

Thoughts of those dark times, when she was property, rose to the forefront of her mind.

It would be easy to think that the beatings, the lashings of a slave girl would linger longest in her mind. But no, more than that, was all the rest. The condescension. The way no one in her whole life treated her like a person of consequence. The way nobody ever asked her for her thoughts in genuine interest.

The way powerful men and women talked as if she were never even there.

All the little ways they undermined her, too. The dry remarks about her heritage and upbringing. The way they callously created work for her by spilling or dropping things without concern, destroying items that cost more than her purchase price just to make her tidy up.

Rage rose up in her at the memories. The long succession of nobles, supervisors, and finally royalty.

A young brat she had to tend to that treated her like her own personal slave. Because she was.

How she wished they could all see her then, atop a hideous throne, with the command of a nation. Able to order their deaths should they cross her realm!

Visions of vengeance flashed through her mind. She envisioned a horrific scene of decapitating the noble woman that had forced Mirella to her knees to clean up priceless wine as she continued her dull chat in the city square. Another memory flooded her of a brutal flogging of the senior servant master that had so casually and nonchalantly implied he would rape her if it pleased him on countless occasions, right there before her and an assemblage of Ariste's finest.

A crack erupted, and Mirella felt a twinge of pain as she broke a finely painted nail upon the throne.

She winced, but was somehow thankful for the reprieve.

Thankful because the dark anger that welled up within her — though maybe related to it — was not the force she was fighting day in, and day out. It was resentment from a life of servitude and abuse. A long lingering force that might've been fueled by her latest conflict, but was borne purely from her.

It was untainted Mirella at its core.

She licked her lips and bit off the broken bit from her nail, fussing about the minor imperfection to her flawless visage. She was Queen — *the* Queen — and she must affect the image of pure beauty and power at all times.

Annoyed with herself and how she'd just lost control, she stared at her finger, willed the damage undone.

And as if a miracle…

She watched as the nail regrew before her very eyes.

It was slow, and at first she doubted what she saw. But in mere minutes she witnessed as her nail grew back to an almost perfect shape… minus the polish.

Mirella was stunned. And more so, as she began to think on how it was possible… she looked inside herself. Felt as if she could feel the very nature of her being on a level she never fathomed.

It was like when she first took over her new form, and her body was all new to her… like her soul donned a fresh new outfit. She felt parts of her inner workings that she never had before then, but she did her best to ignore it. To be comfortable with her new self.

She reeled, her jaw hanging slack as she thought about the implications of her discovery.

If she could heal her broken nail, what else could she accomplish?

And did that explain how she'd recovered so quickly during the assassination attempt that day?

Her world spun, and while she struggled to balance her desire to test its limits with her anxiety over doing something she'd regret, she failed to notice the person who entered her room and now stood before her, agitated.

"Your Majesty!" came a voice, and Mirella had to shake off her stupor.

"Y-yes? What is it?" she said, before she even focussed her gaze to look at the guard before her, and the panting messenger waiting at the door beyond.

"It's the Empire, Your Majesty!" the woman said, eyes wide.

"They're here?" Mirella said in alarm, jerking upwards upon the throne.

"Our outer scouts report that they are on their way and fast approaching!"

"How much time do we have?" Mirella asked tersely.

"Two days at the most, likely closer to one," was the response, and Mirella stood up.

"Send work to all the Raven Guard!" the Queen commanded. "Order all those still lingering outside the walls to take cover in the city, or else retreat with the nomadic tribes to the northern steppes if that is their home."

"Yes, Your Majesty!" snapped the guard in response with a fisted salute.

"Comb the streets for the missing Ambassador, and order all businesses and residences to shutter windows and bar their doors. We are settling in for the long haul," Mirella said as she descended the throne and made way for her antechamber.

"Right away, Your Majesty!" came the final response as the palace burst into a flurry of action.

"Prepare my battle garb," the Queen commanded her handmaiden.

"Right away, Your Majesty," said Yvel, already anxiously awaiting her undoubtedly quick dismissal afterwards.

CHAPTER 27

The renegade witches operated out of a former royal crypt buried in the mountainside. Where once ancient Kings and Queens lay in eternal slumber, Adom watched as a few embittered women plotted and conspired.

It was dark in the hideaway, but thanks to the over-optimistic vision of the former Aristean rulers, the tomb spiralled out into a sprawling catacomb structure that extended into caverns and crevices.

"You should watch out, you could easily get lost down here," cautioned one older woman with grey hair and a wry smirk.

"Ah, thank you," he said, holding a small torch in hand as he peered down one humid crevice, carved out by millennia of water flow.

She said little else as she turned the corner and vanished back towards the main cavern.

He took a bit more time to contemplate his actions.

He placed his trust in Yvel, but still, he didn't like not having any control over his own fate. And the other renegade witches didn't much care for him, speaking little to him, always talking in hushed, muttering voices he couldn't entirely overhear if he tried.

And he did try.

The one thing he could definitely establish was that they were all truly renegades, opposed to the God-King's rule. The one thing he couldn't discern was: why?

With another peering gaze down the water-worn tunnel he pondered his options. Right up until he was disturbed.

"Here you are, after all," came Yvel's familiar voice, the pregnant woman holding a lantern as she studied him.

"I was just exploring my surroundings," he said with a smile before noting the odd assortment of tools she toted in a sack over her shoulder. "What's all this?" he asked of the picks, shovels and hammers.

"Tools we'll need to win a war," she said clearly before pushing past him, her bare, pregnant belly pressing against him as they crossed paths.

"I am no miner or craftsman, I shall warn you," Adom said in mild jest.

"Neither am I," she offered. "But you'll want to come nonetheless."

Adom had learned not to question her too much, and fell into step behind her as she guided the way through the labyrinth of tunnels.

"These crevices must reach all the way down the mountain," he remarked, peering up at the glistening stalactites from which water dripped.

"And all across the city too," she added on.

"You could mount a hit-and-run campaign against the God-King from here," Adom said, in awe at the possibilities.

"That was our thinking when we claimed it. At least, the open possibilities of being able to vanish through one of many exits. They are not as interconnected as we'd like for waging a war, but to flee in desperation? They will do," she remarked, taking him down twists and turns that he could never hope to retrace on his first time.

"Please tell me that is not what we're starting. With hammers and picks no less," he said, his voice dry.

She laughed.

"Today we go to win a war, but not with weapons," she stated cryptically.

"And how do we do that?" his curiosity unquenched.

She let him dangle awhile before answering.

"Your army approaches, Ambassador," she said at last.

Adom's eyes went wide.

"How far away?" he asked anxiously, excited.

"A day away it seems," she said.

"So soon."

"Mmhmm."

"Then how is it we will win this war for the approaching army, my raven beauty?" he asked in amusement.

Though the look she shot back at him said she didn't approve of his claiming ownership of her.

"Well, *my* dear Adom, we are going to tear down the city walls for them. So that they can just march on in," she said both pointedly and confidently.

"Just the two of us? With some picks and hammers? Please tell me there's more to it than that," he said, knowing full well there had to be. Even if he couldn't see it.

She remained silent awhile longer, leading them down the various twists and turns, the sound of running water growing louder as they went.

"The city walls have a single weak point," she said, pausing a moment, listening to the quiet before she led him around a corner.

"And that weak point is?" he asked, playing her game all the way before he came around the corner to see a large underground river that ran from higher up in the mountain, and a makeshift dam that diverted its flow off away from a dirt and rock face that seemed terribly uninteresting but for the wooden buttresses and supports.

She looked back at him with a devious grin.

"The ground beneath them," she said.

CHAPTER 28

Mirella watched from atop her perch overlooking the fields as the Imperial army approached. Ahead of them raced a relatively small band of Ka'reem riders, Raven Guard women skilled with bow and riding.

They raced at breakneck speed as Imperial cavalry attempted to keep up, but failed miserably.

The city gates were left open as the v-shaped formation of Raven Guard riders raced for it. Across the threshold they went, and immediately the mighty doors began to slowly swing shut, as the other layers of protection descended. An iron grating and metal-reinforced wood chiefly.

Down below, Svella descended from her horse, dressed in leathers and silks as all Ka'reem riders did, keeping them protected but light.

The towering northern woman looked up to her Queen upon the walls and quickly ascended, handing her bow to one of the women that tended to her horse.

"How did it go, Svella?" Mirella asked, dressed in a mixture of polished armour and corded leather, decorated with fine clothes stitched with insignias of her station.

"Well, Your Majesty," Svella said, brushing away a stray lock of dark hair. "They were far too numerous to make a serious dent upon them, but we chipped away at their numbers and hopefully made them feel frustratingly impotent."

Mirella looked aside at her friend and cracked a smirk.

"It should hopefully hurt morale, and make them all the more on edge when what few riders from the north we have left sweep in to occasionally pick at them," Mirella said, her long blonde hair trapped within a mail hood, upon which her circlet rested.

"Yes, the few small bands of raiders we have in the northern steppes have pledged to raid routinely. Their numbers are very small, and they are almost all old women, but they are skilled in the Ka'reem bow. They can move fast and stay out of range of the Imperials while pelting a few arrows."

Mirella locked her jaw firmly into place and nodded.

"Thank the Northern Skies for the ingenuity of Ka'reem craftwork," Mirella said, watching the sprawling mass of the Imperial army plodding towards them.

At last the cavalry began to close in, only to wheel about and scurry away back towards the main forces long before they entered into Aristean bow range.

"It shall be a long war, Svella. I can feel it," Mirella said, her white-fur lined cloak blowing in the wind.

CHAPTER 29

The city closed down as people shut themselves in, the beginning of the siege a slow and dreary affair as both forces prepared.

"What say we liven things up, Your Majesty?" came the grinning cry from the Queen's battle engineer.

"Yes, see to it that the Empire has no peace as they set up camp," Mirella responded.

The Aristean woman wore a padded jerkin and a giddy grin.

"You know, Your Majesty, I was never allowed to study my craft in the old days," the engineer said as she used coloured flags to signal her crews about the city, positioned upon rooftops and city walls all about.

"Then now is your chance to shine, Laurilae. Let it hail," the Queen declared, still upon the outer walls while the Empire was safely out of range, their own ballistas not yet set up.

With a final flick of her wrists, Laurilae summoned the start of her efforts, then turned to the crew just within earshot.

"You heard the Queen! Show these dogs the cost of renting our front stoop!" Laurilae shouted.

"Excitable woman, Your Majesty," Svella said with a wry grin.

"You sound like you appreciate her qualities, dear friend," Mirella said, just before the show began.

It was still day as the Imperial Army set up camp, spanning the whole vista within the frame of the mountain ridges. Their own workers quickly set about assembling their ballistas and catapults, but Aristae was there first.

And better.

The trebuchets upon the parapets let fly without human muscle, and even though the Queen's keen sense of hearing detected Laurilae's nervous muttering of "please work, please work" she only smirked wider. And watched.

It looked so simple, but unlike the Imperial siege weapons, which required slave muscle to power, Ariste's new weapons were powered by the genius of that one exuberant woman.

Well, her and the witches.

The payload carried out to the siege forces, reaching their limit exactly as Laurilae promised.

Though the curious ceramic payload had no noticeable effect. At first, that is.

It hit the ground, smashing open and casting its noxious fluid all about, one after another.

"I appreciate her results," Svella said with a firm nod, but a glance aside at the exuberant Laurilae who jumped in victorious rejoicing.

The shattered payloads took a while to kick in, but then abruptly flashes of colour began to light up the enemy forces, and Imperial soldiers — far off in the distance — began to stagger and lurch.

"Reload!" Cried Laurilae, before turning her attention back to the two women. "So what does that stuff do anyhow?"

"A few things," Svella said, taking a subtle cue from Mirella in the form of a nod to explain. "One, it stinks," she said, and it became easy to see how many of them were gagging and covering their mouths to little avail.

"I can see that. But surely that's not the most destructive part," Laurilae said.

"Two, it induces vomiting and queasiness that lasts for up to days," Svella continued, undaunted.

"How… insidious," Laurilae responded as her workers all across the city reloaded for another blast.

"Thirdly, it draws carrion beasts to them," Svella said, nodding to the skies, noting the flocks of birds that seemed to be zeroing in upon the Imperial forces. "The flash of light you just witnessed was like a summons they cannot turn down. And they shall pester the Empire for weeks, picking at their wounded and vulnerable and making off with their supplies."

"I cannot decide whether it is a rather crude device, or an especially elegant weapon of war," Mirella remarked.

"That's all it does, though? It doesn't kill anyone?" Laurilae asked.

"Why kill a handful when we could wound and weaken more? Then force even more to tend to and protect the wounded? Besides, some always die from natural diseases anyhow, this will only help it along," Svella explained.

"I see…" Laurilae said, mulling it all over.

"It shall be a long war, Battle Engineer. Reducing the enemy's effectiveness is quite valuable indeed. The more of them we keep off the battlefield, the longer we delay them, the more of our lives we save," Mirella said confidently.

Without needing further command, the next barrage was launched in time.

A third volley even managed to hit before the Empire could muster its forces to withdraw and set up camp an extra distance back, out of Ariste's more advanced weaponry.

Disaster, however, was not far behind.

CHAPTER 30

Mirella still stood on watch over the city, issuing commands to her troops and overseeing the defense of Ariste when the wall came down.

From high above the city, upon the inner walls surrounding the palace, she — like everyone else — found her gaze drawn by the terrible sound of stone cracking, crumbling and caving in.

Thousands stood in shocked silence as, seemingly without any interference from the Empire, a section of the beautiful white-stone wall fell in the east. Dust and debris went up into the air as stones fell, some impacting nearby buildings, and a few guards who manned the wall went plummeting to their inevitable death or grievous injury.

Mirella stared wide-eyed and shocked as the first moments of surprise they'd delivered to the Empire were undone right before her eyes. An unexpected twist that compromised everything.

"What just happened?" Mirella muttered.

Svella moved up beside her, her mouth agape.

"What are your orders, Your Majesty?" she asked as the Raven's Guard women crowded around, staring and waiting.

A crumpled mess was left once the dust cleared. The wall was mostly still intact but that one gap left a gaping vulnerability that could only be filled in with the lives of the Queen's soldiers, which were still in limited supply.

"Your Majesty?" Svella asked, shaking the Queen's arm, the action taking Mirella back into the moment and out of the deadlock of worry in her mind.

"Order the Heron Clan's women down there immediately!" Mirella commanded brusquely. "Svella! Open the gates and launch another sortie out! We should be able to get the gates shut in time for your return, and if not… we've already got one gap, another won't make things much worse."

"Aye, my Queen!" Svella said, rushing off.

"Get me Inyis this instant!" Mirella snapped to her entourage of waiting Raven's Guard.

The city was abuzz and it took the guards a while to track down the officer Inyis, but there she turned up inevitably, panting and out of breath.

"Your Majesty," she said, bowing before the Queen.

"You said the wall would hold for now!" the Queen said, anger in her eyes as she jabbed a finger at the woman.

Inyis looked wide-eyed and shocked.

"The masons all assured me it would, Your Majesty! They—" the Queen cut her off.

"Well clearly it hasn't! And it couldn't have possibly failed on us at a worse time! Do you realize what this oversight has cost us? Do you?" the Queen shouted shrilly, her arm trembling with barely repressed rage as she wished to lash out at the woman.

Everyone was silent and went rigidly still. Not a one around was unaware of the just how far the Queen's temper had flared.

Inyis, however, the source of all that ire, held strong. Squaring her shoulders, she did not challenge the Queen but held her ground firmly, passively.

"The mason's know their craft, Your Majesty. If they have erred, and I have erred for trusting their judgment, then our punishment is in your hands," she said, standing there, as if awaiting her execution upon the spot.

However, Battle Engineer Laurilae stepped forward and spoke up.

"Your Majesty," she said, bowing her head to her Queen, hand to her chest. She received no direct go ahead to speak, but the Queen's prolonged silence seemed to say enough. "The timing of all this is circumspect."

"What do you mean?" Mirella said, speaking through the cloud of rage in her mind.

The women all looked at each other, letting the idea sink in.

"That collapse was imminent as is, but should not have been a threat for years without pressure from assault. The fact that it happened now, just as our enemy was setting up camp… it is suspicious," Laurilae said, taking a step back after offering her knowledgeable opinion.

The thought of treason incensed part of her, but that had the effect of putting two halves at war within Mirella's mind. And that gave her enough of a stalemate to find calm and resume command more effectively.

"Laurilae and Inyis!" she commanded sharply. "Go see to some emergency repairs to the wall."

"That would take mon—" Inyis was cut off by the Queen.

"I know! I'm not asking you to rebuild it! Think up something and think it up fast! Plug that gap, give our soldiers something to take up positions behind!" she commanded.

"Perhaps…" Laurilae began, rubbing her chin.

"Think as you move ladies! We need action **now**!" Mirella commanded.

Inyis and Laurilae rushed on down the city streets, muttering to each other possible ideas.

Mirella turned to her guards, fanned around her.

"Rally as many people as possible to provide the support they need. Rouse commoners from their homes to help lift stones and bridge that gap! Move!" she commanded.

The moments after that ticked by agonizingly slowly, yet all too fast despite it.

"Any movement from the Imperial Army?" Mirella asked as she rode down the main thoroughfare of Ariste towards the walls once more.

"No, Your Majesty. They are oddly still. No signs of setting up camp even," reported the guardswoman at her side.

"They must be concerned that this is a feint to lure them in again," Mirella said, thinking it all over. "Make sure all the trebuchets are ready to fire the moment they start moving in again! Don't put too many archers on the walls, withdraw some of those we have there already. Make it look like we've got less power."

Mirella came closer to the front gates, where Svella and her troops were acquiring fresh horses after their last sortie.

"For the God-King!" Mirella shouted to her comrade, and the women raised their bows as the gates started to move.

Veering off to the right, Mirella made her way towards the broken section of the wall. There, in the streets she found Inyis and Laurilae commanding the masons and workers, pulling some barricades from the main road to the side.

"Why aren't you working on the wall itself?" the Queen demanded imperiously.

"We had an idea, Your Majesty," Laurilae said.

The Queen bristled, but Mirella forced calm and nodded. "Speak!" she demanded.

"No work we could do on the wall would make it as impervious as it once was, Your Majesty," Laurilae stated definitively.

"But any attempts we make to bar the gap will be apparent and targeted by the Empire, to inevitably be bashed through. It is only a matter of time," Inyis added.

"Right. So Inyis proposed something," Laurilae said, looking to the other woman.

"We leave the gap with only a minor barricade, but then we commandeer the buildings on this side, construct a new cul-de-sac fortification," Inyis stated.

Mirella's eyes widened.

"Yes… and so as they funnel through…" Mirella said.

"We reap them like the summer harvest," Laurilae said proudly.

"They won't be able to see what we hide on this side of the wall, after all. And their troops won't know until they're already pushing over the wall," Inyis explained.

"But how long will we be able to hold that line?" Mirella asked.

The two women looked to one another before Inyis spoke up.

"Not forever. But there is no perfect solution, Your Majesty."

CHAPTER 31

Dusk was approaching as Svella led her raid back towards the gates, though with the Empire not daring to pursue, things were quieter than anticipated. The defense preparations worked through the night, and Mirella found herself unable to sleep.

No less because she spent her entire night both worrying about the course of battle and trying to reach out to Kulav once more, to no avail.

As dawn broke over the city, she summoned her commanders for a meeting in the cool morning air overlooking the city. Off in the distance, the campfires of the Imperial Army burned.

"How go all operations?" Mirella asked.

"The sortie was tough," Svella reported first of all. "The Empire was not playing with us, and held their ground firmly. I believe they expect it and the collapsed wall were both part of some attempt to lure them into a trap, Your Majesty."

Mirella nodded.

"And of the rest of you?" she enquired.

"The buildings around the gap have been commandeered and fortified," Laurilae said. "We have done what we can to make them into fortified bunkers, using windows as points for archers."

"We have our finest Raven's Guard women manning the breach, Your Majesty. They will hold that ground for as long as possible, and give their lives to keep the enemy at bay," Inyis stated and the Raven's Guard all saluted and bowed their heads in honour of the sacrifice that was to come.

Mirella, however, was not so keen.

"I am not fond of the idea of sacrificing our very best for momentary gain," Mirella stated, catching the eyes of all around, who were quite surprised by the sudden change.

"What would you ask of us, Your Majesty? Surrender the city?" Svella said, sounding surprised by the Queen's tone.

"No, of course not. But offer slivers of the city as needed, at great cost," Mirella stated firmly and confidently.

"I have been up all night thinking about it," she stated, explaining to the confused faces around her. "If the fortifications are prepared at the gap now, I want workers to start making secondary barriers right behind them. Then a third line, and so on."

Slowly the women's eyes began to light up as they understood her meaning.

"We hold each line of defense as long as possible, turn each cul-de-sac into a river of blood until the line can be held no longer. Whereupon our women retreat back to the next line and start the whole process over again," Mirella said.

"Each victory of theirs would be but a refresher of our defensive position," Inyis said.

"Precisely. Just as they think they have won a breakthrough, we'll have fallen back to a more defensible position, ready and waiting for them," Mirella said.

"We must get to work on that immediately, Your Majesty. It is a genius plan, but each new barrier will require more work than the last," Laurilae said. "Each one will necessarily be larger than the last as we sacrifice city blocks and their hold enlarges."

"Very well. Start right away," Mirella said.

"We should have workers going around the clock in shifts," Inyis said. "We have bodies from the citizenry, and only so many can work at any one section at a time. We can get more use from them like this as we gather clutter from the mountain."

"Your Majesty," said the woman, bowing and saluting as was appropriate for their respective ranks before then scurrying off to work.

Everything was moving so quickly, dawn light had barely hit before the Imperial Army finally took to the move.

"They've decided we're too irresistible a target, after all," Svella said as she watched the seemingly endless forces of the Empire begin to move.

"They have two options: wait us out or push and potentially end this now. If they wait us out as we appear vulnerable, their commander's forces will grow antsy, and begin to doubt their leadership," Mirella said.

"An astute observation," Svella said. "Of course they risk falling into a trap this way. But regardless... they must be confident in their ability to withstand the losses."

"They have ample numbers to," Mirella stated the obvious, anxious about it all.

It was too true. No matter how much hurt she could inflict upon the Empire, she hadn't the forces to truly defeat them. The most she could do was buy time, whittle them down and maybe weaken them for the God-King's arrival.

The Imperial army seemed to crawl across the fields, but once it hit the threshold of Ariste's trebuchets the projectiles went flying. All across the city, weaponry sprung to action, flinging vile weapons at the approaching army.

On they came anyhow, their own catapults sticking up amidst their forces as they approached the wall. Many of their soldiers fell, vomiting and sick, but on the tide came uninterrupted, countless more to replace them.

At a certain point, the Empire's catapults stopped and then the retaliatory stones went flying. The heavy projectiles crashed into the stonework of the city, mostly causing minor damage, but here and there Mirella could see homes with holes bashed in.

Once they reached the range of the Ka'reem bows, the sky turned dark.

"It is like the skies in summer, when the black flies swarm out of the forests," Svella remarked in the moment before the arrows finished their arc and descended from the sky into the Imperial Army.

Bodies fell in greater numbers than ever, and the next volley came on fast, as more archers rushed to the walls, sending another hail.

It took the Empire longer to get in range of their own bows, but once they did… the hail of arrows made the Ka'reem barrage seem piddling by comparison. For the soldiers in the thick of it, it was as if the sun were blotted out.

Ka'reem fighters wore much lighter armour than their Imperial counterparts, but the city walls and barricades provided better defense. On and on the battle went, arrows traded from side to side, until at last the Imperial forces reached the walls themselves.

Heavily armed soldiers took up positions, lifting ladders to the walls, or rushing into the gap.

Imperial soldiers on the front line came as a phalanx, heavy shields out front as they advanced into the city. Their defensive armour, however, could not protect them entirely, and as they got into the cul-de-sac Ka'reem warriors began to cut them down.

From her perch above, Mirella watched it all, tensely grasping the stonework.

The true weakness was that as the Imperial soldiers attempted to climb the stonework or barricades, they left themselves open to the Raven's Guard women plunging spears or arrows into them.

"It shall be a long battle, Mirella," Svella muttered.

CHAPTER 32

The first barrier fell by the second day, but before the day was out, it was reclaimed.

Svella reported the back and forth results to Mirella as the days wore on, but one thing was unavoidable: the Empire was pushing in.

A week in and the first barrier was long gone, the second coming soon after.

"Once they take the fifth barrier, an access point to the wall itself will open. They will be able to put pressure upon our archers. It will be a problem," Svella reported.

"Equip the workers with mining picks, tear down the steps there, bit by it," Mirella ordered.

Just like those stairs, bit by bit the city was being disassembled. A whole quarter of the city was marked as off-limits to civilians, except to workers.

That was where line after line of defensive positions was prepared. All planned as an eventual sacrifice to the defense.

Staring down at the city, the Queen felt flashbacks to the first time she met the God-King. Ariste was on fire then, now it was battered, busted, broken and reassembled in a hasty fashion.

Ariste now, however, fought back still, unlike that night years ago.

The trebuchets still fired, even if they were long out of that concoction and now merely hurled stones from the mountain. The archers still flung arrows. The guards still made the Empire pay for every inch of Ariste.

"How much ground have we given to the enemy?" Mirella asked, no longer watching over the parapets, but snugly inside her throne room, safe from the Empire's catapults.

"The Empire has now claimed numerous city blocks," Inyis stated. "We make them pay for each, and momentarily push them back. But ultimately they are advancing, and we haven't the numbers to stop them."

"Yes, but how much?" Mirella insisted.

"Nearly the full quarter of the city," Laurilae stated.

Mirella's pregnant belly was swollen larger, the daughter that grew within her — and she willed it to be a daughter, like she willed her nail to repair that time — compelling her to strive harder. She had to make it, so that Kulav could return and be gifted this child.

"How long until we expect the God-King's return?" Mirella asked, focussing on herself. Keeping calm.

Despite the stress of the period, she was finding it easier to keep the intruding presence of that other consciousness out of her mind. She could rule more effectively as Mirella than the Queen, and she was grateful for the release of that pressure.

Fighting a battle in herself as she sought to win a war was more trying than she could hope to contend with, she felt.

"It could be a month… or more, Your Majesty," Svella said.

"That long?" Mirella asked, bothered.

"Or he could be here any time now," Inyis added.

"Yes, but we have not received any raven's carrying word of his victory. So I would err on the side of caution, Your Majesty," Svella urged, her battle clothes showing signs of wear and tear, after having commanded directly at the breach numerous times.

"We simply can't count on his prompt return," Laurilae said, summing up the other woman's words before heaving a sigh.

"Let us rest assured at least that for the time being, we can hold down the home front. Our usual advantages mean less in this situation, our horses and bows aren't as effective in this close street fighting. But the Queen's deft recruitment of local volunteers ahead of time means we will have troops enough to spare for the growing battle front," Svella said confidently.

"Should worse come to worst, we could abandon the lower half of the city entirely. The old city walls will then form a more than adequate barricade against the intruders," Inyis stated.

"Then, ladies, let us keep an ever vigilant watch. The God-King shall have a momentous task in rooting out these intruders upon his return, as is. Let's ensure events do not spiral out of control any further," Mirella said, feeling more upbeat as she took control of her own being more securely. A genuine smile even managed to form upon her face, regardless of the reasons for why she no longer faced the inner resistance.

"Events are under our control, Your Majesty. We need only buy time whereas the Empire needs to take the whole city before the God-King returns," stated Svella.

CHAPTER 33

The street fighting carried on relentlessly, what were once peaceful homes were now the battleground between heavily armoured Imperial phalanxes and spry Raven's Guardswomen. The battle-hardened women had been raised for the fight, they were however new to this kind of warfare.

When the Ka'reem had seized the city the first time, the God-King had done so with such swiftness and surprise that there had been no organized defense. Under cover of night they had rode in, taken the gates and swept through the city, hemming what few soldiers that remained into their garrisons.

It was a different kind of war they were waging, and a different kind of leader in charge.

Mirella's own force of Aristeans were well-trained by now, or as well-trained as any could become without actual war experience. And they were set to march into the battle.

For that, however, she had decided to lead them herself.

"You should not put yourself in harm's way, Your Majesty," Svella objected as she watched the Queen stretch and perform a ritualistic form of exercise that her warrior-concubine sisters had taught her.

The fluid motions were both graceful and practical, stretching limbs and preparing muscles.

Mirella also found that they helped her focus her abilities upon her flesh, helping her prepare her body. Pregnancy slowed her, made her bulkier, but she was intent upon operating at her best. No, better than her best.

So while Svella attempted to talk her out of it, Mirella focussed her mind, could visualize her body and being. She felt the fiber and sinew that made up her muscles and willed them to grow stronger.

She was a slight woman, but already in the time since full war was upon them, she had — through nearly sheer force of mystical will alone — grown more agile and leanly muscled. It helped change her appearance, making her look harder, more powerful, all while maintaining an air of regal elegance.

"Your Majesty?" Svella said again, unable to pierce Mirella's deep concentration.

The city outside still sounded with the crash of stones hurled to and fro, the sound of booted feet rushing hither and thither. But Mirella balanced upon one set of toes as she lifted another leg up, and up, until it touched her up-stretched fingers.

She wore little, a gauzy smock that dangled down between her legs and covered — but did not hide — her upper body, her pale form showing the light signs of sculpted muscle beneath her soft skin. All her attempts to reach out to Kulav again had failed, and she would not let herself think of the worst, only prepare. Hone what skills she had and settle in for the greatest test of her life thus far.

More than simply stretching and performing, she leapt, twisted, spun about in the air and mimed fencing maneuvers. She reached into her mind, drawing upon lessons past of how to fight with weapon and without. She mimicked the maneuvers with speed and precision like never before.

Like perhaps no other in the city could challenge.

"Mirella?" Svella said, at last pulling the woman out of her trance-like state.

"Yes, my friend?" Mirella asked, her voice soft even if her body was less so.

Svella was silent, however.

"You were saying?" Mirella asked, turning to see the woman staring with wide-eyed surprise.

"How did you do all of that?" she asked, the tall, strong woman — with a physique that still appeared visually the superior but — who was shown a display of strength, agility and prowess that had undone her limits.

"Practice," Mirella said simply with a teasing, uneven smile.

"No I'm serious… how?" she said, clearly not buying into the simple explanation.

Mirella strode softly over upon her bare feet towards the rack on the wall, plucking up a towel for herself after dismissing all of her servants.

"It's… complicated, Svella," she said.

"I am certain! But what you just did… pregnant or no, it shouldn't be possible," Svella said, shaking her head in disbelief.

"I have been focussing my powers, Svella. Discovering… new ways to do things," Mirella explained, wiping away the dewy sweat from her pale form.

"The magic of the sisterhood is not to be trifled with so lightly, my friend," Svella said in a dire warning.

"No. I know, Svella. It's not that," she said, thinking it over. "The source of this power isn't the same. It's… from within."

Svella stepped closer, sizing her up closely.

"I don't understand… how can there be another source?" she asked.

Mirella had to think about it, as it was something she'd avoided pondering on too much.

"When I claimed for myself a new skin… something changed," Mirella said.

"How so?"

"It was like… my soul was no longer quite fitted to my body. It no longer fit like a perfect glove. It meant that I could feel the contours, imperfections and differences in the skin I wore. I could detect nuance in my being the way I never could in the body I was born to," Mirella explained.

Svella's eyes were still wide, seeming stunned by the information.

"For awhile it troubled me greatly. But when I realized I could use that knowledge to control aspects of my body like never before... that I could access parts of myself like some people can twitch an ear or nostrils, while others can't seem to isolate the muscles to do so... a whole new avenue for improvement opened up before me."

Mirella, finished her explanation, looked to Svella to find her still staring with that awed look.

"Have I troubled you, my friend? Have I done something wrong? Was this some taboo brought on my by acts?" Mirella asked.

Svella shook her head, slowly wiping the look from her face.

"No. No, not that I know of, Mirella. I just... I just don't know what to say. This is... this is the stuff of legendary tales," she said, a cautious smile forming upon her face.

Mirella laughed and tossed her towel into a heap by the rack.

"Don't go condemning me to tales and history just yet, my friend. I still have much to do to earn my sp—" her words were cut off when a sudden rumbling shook the floor, nay, the whole palace.

Svella and Mirella held onto one another's arms as the whole world moved about them. It didn't last too long, but once it stopped, they looked at each other with worry.

"What was that?" Mirella asked.

Svella swallowed nervously.

"I don't know, my friend, but we should go out and see."

Without taking time to dress, the two strode out of the palace, past confused guards and alarmed servants. There on the palace walls, they saw guards crowded around, watching.

"What's happened?" Svella asked one of the women as they mounted the stairs to peer out over the city.

"We don't know, ma'am," said the guard, who only belatedly seemed to notice Mirella and bow. "Your Majesty."

They all looked out over the city in confusion, until another rumble quaked the mountain itself. There, behind and to the right, near the palace itself, some stones tumbled from the mountain, crashing to the ground noisily.

It lasted longer, but ultimately ended the same as before.

The two women looked at one another.

"People may take this as a bad sign. The mountain, the earth itself, displeased with us," Svella warned her Queen.

Mirella mulled it over and nodded.

"We must allay their fears... somehow," Mirella said.

"We must gather the sisters of the coven, and seek some answers. It is the only thing we might do," Svella said, knowing full well what she proposed.

And the potential costs of doing so.

CHAPTER 34

Mirella entered into the dark chamber of the coven, the women — young and old — who were at the highest echelons of the Raven Guard. The warrior-concubines who wielded sorcery beyond understanding.

They all donned ceremonial garb, with ash marked upon their faces, feathers knit into their hair.

"Sisters," Mirella began, knowing that these were the only women who knew who she truly was. All knew she had wielded their magic before, albeit in a different body. "The God-King requires sacrifice from us. The mountain quakes and enemies are in our midst. We must take action," she said before sitting down at the head of the table.

The women looked around, pondering such radical action. One woman spoke up first.

"Is it not premature to summon such powers? The hour is not so dark as that, is it?" she asked.

"The cost last time we called upon our sorcery was… dear," another woman added with a nod.

"Yes, I am aware, sisters. And I do not ask that we shake the mountain, nor even cease the mountain from shaking. But that we merely find out… why, and what we might do about it in mortal means," Mirella said.

"These quakes have been breaking morale, and making people — both Ka'reem and Aristean — lose faith," Svella said. "We must provide answers at the very least."

The women looked about and slowly they began to nod.

"Very well," Mirella said, holding out her two hands to each side, Svella taking one. "We shall not risk too much this time. We only ask for a little."

As all the women joined hands and the ritual humming began, the energy between them began to mount as the hums became chanting.

The physical world seemed to slip away, as if the floor dropped out from beneath them but they remained suspended in air.

Darkness filled the room, seeming to suffocate the candles and sconces. The smell of incense became something otherworldly, scents that were alien to life of the mortal realm.

Their consciousness's joined together, as they had years ago, and they sought answers from the fabric of reality itself.

Mirella felt herself as helmswoman of their journey, guiding them through what was both nothingness and everything, through reality and the spaces in between.

The mountain itself was not the mountain as they knew it, but seemed as if a bright light. Lifeless stone was blinding brightness of a million pinprick points of light.

She guided them, seeking their answers... seeking the truth...

But neither lay within the mountain itself.

Truth lay beyond.

Easier than altering reality or telling the future, seeking out knowledge from the now was one of the simplest of tasks the coven could do. Yet it was not without costs and risks. Mirella found such an unexpected cost when — as she stretched out their combined presence to the other side of the mountain — she encountered a hostile force.

A malevolence of unexpected presence met them in challenge, pushed them back so that they went spiralling through the mountain and back into their physical beings.

All of a sudden reality rushed back at them, the floor hard and cool, present beneath them once more. Air filling their lungs, pressing in upon them.

Many gasped, some bowed over and vomited, paying the price for the group. Mirella and Svella were among the lucky ones who seemed to exhibit no cost for their sorcery.

But all began to look around.

"What was that?" was the question on more than one woman's lips.

"I don't know," said Mirella.

But it was all too familiar.

CHAPTER 35

Yvel watched as other sisters of the inner coven were led out of a private meeting chamber and back to the rest. Some were clearly sick, or weak. Signs of having used their powers.

She traded glances with some of the other women, those who shared in their secret plots.

It took them a while, but eventually, one by one, they filtered off, away from the rest and reconvened back in the catacombs. Yvel made her way there first, finding Adom waiting for her.

"What's going on?" he asked, noticing her pensive look.

"I don't know yet," she stated.

Finally, once all were together they began.

"They were conjuring spells. In secret," said the oldest of the group.

"Without the rest of us," Yvel added.

Adom only stood by, barely able to believe what he was hearing. To cast spells like that was something only spoken of in myths and legends in the south. Madness at best, perhaps.

"This is unheard of," another woman said, sounding indignant.

"They cast those spells without you all during the war," Yvel said to the older women.

"That was different. Each of us was away or sick, then," one of them explained. "Mirella did not exclude us then, as the God-King's chief consort. But the Queen has the nerve to do so now, when the situation is dire."

Of course, they didn't understand the truth. Not a single one of them knew that Mirella and the Queen were one in the same. For them, Mirella was a folk-hero, a woman from humble origins as a slave, who earned the right to be one of the Raven's Guard through hard work and loyalty, who won the heart of the God-King.

She was a symbol of all that a normal woman could accomplish.

But her arrest and banishment destroyed all that.

"Why though? Nothing has changed," Yvel said. "We saw no signs of magic today. The mountain still trembles off and on. What were they doing that required this… secrecy? Why are we not trusted?"

A suspicious look went through the women like wildfire.

"Does the Queen suspect us?" asked one woman to Yvel's right.

Worried mutters broke out until Yvel spoke up.

"We should cast our own conjuring! Trace their steps and find out what it was that they sought. If we are under suspicion, we must act quickly or else be sacrifices to the Queen's ever growing power," she said.

The women took just a moment to nod their heads and agree.

"Into the rear cave," commanded the eldest woman.

As they began to filter out, Adom touched Yvel's arm to stop her first.

"Why does this woman Mirella matter so much to you all, anyhow? Why is it you're all willing to commit treason, to undo your own people's conquest of this city?" he asked, the question burning in his mind for so long.

Yvel looked at him as if he were daft, a complete moron.

With brow furrowed, she said, "Because there must be justice. Because the world is not fair, it is devoid of value and meaning, except for that which we give it. And all in the coven are taught from youth that we must be harbingers of justice and equity. And Mirella is as our living Saint. If the God-King cannot respect the offerings of her loyalty and sacrifice, then he is not a ruler fit to lead, and the people who follow him are not deserving of victory."

She pulled away from him and strode into the next room.

There the women gathered around a circle as some lit sconces and candles.

Their conjuring went much as the other one not long before. The world slipping away from them as they ventured forth.

They followed after the trail of the other witches, through the mountain… right into the grasp of that malevolent force. It met them with just as much rage and animosity as the others, but they persisted.

They persisted until all at once, their eyes shot open in realization.

In realization of what was coming. Who was coming.

Their help was needed.

CHAPTER 36

Mirella donned her battle garb with the aid of her assistants, minus the absent Yvel.

"I still think this is an unwise move, Your Majesty," Svella said, formal in front of the others. "Without you we are a wolf without its head. A pack without its leader."

Mirella smiled at the other woman as her assistants strapped the metal and leather into place, garnishing it with frilly lace and silks in the lavish custom of the royal house.

"I will not die, Svella. And our people need some inspiration right now. They need to see that we are strong, that I have confidence in them and our situation. The Raven's Guard women are stretched too thin, and are in need of relief. Once they see their Queen riding into battle with relief forces, things will look that much better," Mirella said in a smooth, honeyed voice, brimming with confidence that she wasn't sure she felt.

"And where is that handmaiden of yours anyhow? Shouldn't she be here for this?" Svella asked, looking at the intricate work going into Mirella's dressing.

"I think she's perhaps gotten the hint, she lingers around less and less," Mirella confessed.

"You are too harsh," Svella said with a softly chastising voice and a mild smile.

"You are perhaps right, old friend. Bu—" a loud thunderous cry seemed to split the air and quake the ground.

"What now…?" Mirella muttered, rushing to the balcony overlooking the courtyard outside.

There below was the new legion of Aristean warriors awaiting her address, but what had their and everyone's attention was that sound, and the effect it had upon the mountain.

Rocks shook loose from the mountain face, boulders crashed into the marble palace in places, causing devastation, but there… at the former tunnel, left blocked from the previous war…

It shook more than anything else. Stones dislodged, seemed to jump and rocket through the air.

"What is going on?!" Svella shouted, shocked by it all.

Though the only answer was the explosion of force that sent stones flying through the air from out of that tunnel, a blast that caused mayhem and destruction. The cry of rage only dying off once its work was done and the way was clear, clear but for the dust.

"The tunnel is open! The Empire!" Svella shouted, wide-eyed and panicked. "How could those southerners wield such force?!"

Mirella watched as the situation grew all the more dire, a new battlefront opened up, their situation gotten all the worse in the blink of an eye.

"The Empire is going to be coming through any moment," Mirella said, clutching the railing. "Rally!" She cried.

Despite her swollen belly, she vaulted over the railing and down into the courtyard below.

"About face! Everyone!" she screamed, motioning with her arms. "To the breach! We must defend our city! Meet them head on!"

The freshly trained soldiers were still dumbfounded, but their Queen's commanding cries got them into shape. Not all at once, but as their formations started the rest fell into line. Their training fresh, they marched from the courtyard, and Svella climbed slowly down the wall to join her Queen.

"We'll show them that no surprise is enough to stand against us!" Mirella cried, moving to the center to command her troops.

They marched towards the tunnel as the dust slowly cleared, and none too soon, as on the other side they could see: a mass of heavily armoured troops marching slowly down towards them.

CHAPTER 37

Yvel's vision was blurry, the world spun around her.

She had never before joined with the sisters to summon forth their mystical power, and the effects were… jarring.

She knew there was a cost, and that was why they joined together, to share the burden and lessen the loss to them all. But she felt like she was drunk, drugged and sick all at once. The world was mute to her, she couldn't feel anything except nausea.

Her vision worked, but it was a confusing jumble of actions and angles.

Looking about she could see other women, sick like her, some others… far worse.

One woman was a bloody, twitching mess. Another lay absolutely still, eyes open.

They had cast a powerful spell to clear the mountain, and the cost would always be proportionate.

Just as the world started to steady, suddenly she felt herself rising up. It took her a moment to realize it was Adom helping her to her feet, taking her away from the ring of women.

"What just happened?!" she finally managed to hear him say through the mental haze. "Are you alright?!" he asked, looking her over with an obvious concern that made her grin unevenly despite her situation.

"We opened the way," she muttered as he carried her to a cozy mat at the side.

"Opened the way to what?" he asked, confused.

"Not what… who," she stated.

"Who? Opened the way to who?" he asked insistently.

CHAPTER 38

The cavernous tunnel echoed with the blaring trumpets of the Empire, but above the mass of troops, one figure stood alone.

"Who is that?" Svella asked breathlessly, already knowing in her heart who it was.

Mirella swallowed anxiously, for she knew it not only in her heart, or her bones, but in the being of her soul. She felt this woman's approach before anyone else. Thirst for revenge drove her on, and somehow she had found the instruments.

"It's her," was all she could manage to say though, her pace continuing as her new legion continued into the tunnel.

"Her? Her who?!" Svella asked.

"Annabelle," Mirella said, looking at her friend wide-eyed and anxious.

There she was, the former Princess Annabelle Flair, now inhabiting the body of Mirella, stood upon a palanquin carried by Imperial soldiers.

Svella's eyes went wide and she shouted out loudly.

"Sound the horns!" Svella said.

Mirella took over there, pushing aside guilt and worry to take command.

"Raise your shields! Raise the bows in back and prepare to fire!" she commanded her Aristean forces, wearing a mix of the Ka'reem light armour and the more southern style of heavy shields and spears.

The new soldiers carried out their orders with precision however, their Ka'reem task-masters proving to be able teachers, and many of them sticking on to be unit commanders of the Aristeans even then.

The two forces marched on until the Queen shouted.

"Halt! Assume positions!" She was just beyond the mouth of the cavern. "Let them wear themselves out marching on us," she said.

Though waiting was torturous.

The cavern inhibited the archers, but waiting where they were, Mirella hoped to give themselves an advantage.

"Hold fire until my command!" she cried out, though her eyes were focussed upon the visage of her foe in her former body.

She could see the woman so crystal clear despite the distance, see her clenched teeth, flared nostrils and wild eyes. She was driven mad with rage.

It was too late that she realized Annabelle was inside her mind though, that she was seeing her so clearly because she was assaulting her from across that gap. They waged a war of minds, but Mirella was at a disadvantage, taken by surprise as she was.

As the Imperial troops entered into range Svella looked to Mirella, surprised by the lack of order. Then she noticed the glassy eyed stare upon her friend's face. Shaking her had no effect, though it was the last thing Mirella remembered of the battle.

CHAPTER 39

Mirella awoke with a start, finding herself upon a cot in a lowly barracks, rather than the posh bed of her palace suite.

She was breathing heavily, but immediately she saw familiar faces coming towards her.

"Your Majesty!" said one of the servant girls who tended her, looking utterly relieved.

"Where is Svella?" Mirella asked promptly, without delay.

"She is resting from overseeing the fight. There is a momentary lull at the tunnel, last I heard," the young woman explained in a soft, even voice.

"I need to see her," Mirella said, pushing herself up to a sitting position.

"Yes, Your Majesty," she said, bowing and running off.

Though one of the healers approached her quickly after.

"Take it easy, Your Majesty! You are pregnant and you have not been responsive for some time. Here," said the woman, handing her some water and gently helping her drink it.

"What's your name again?" Mirella asked, finding the woman's presence soothing.

"Soralin," she said with a gentle smile.

"Right," Mirella said, her memory coming back to her. "You were Fourth Healer to the God-King's mother," she said.

"You never forget anyone, do you, Your Majesty?" she said with a smile, making way as Svella came rushing into the room.

"Your Majesty! You're okay!" Svella said with relief, immediately dropping to her knees and clasping Mirella's hands. She wore only a simply tunic and boots, that she had apparently worn to bed before the interruption.

"I'm fine, Svella," Mirella said calmly, feeling a little overwhelmed. "Tell me... how is the battle going? I heard we are still holding at the tunnel? Is it true?" she asked, concern clearly written upon her face as she rested one arm about her pregnant belly.

"Yes, we are holding, Your Majesty," she said, her shoulders seeming to relax from the heavy burden they carried now that she was back to consciousness. "We have held the tunnel for a full week."

"A week?!" Mirella said, astonished and horrified at being out of commission so long.

"Yes," Svella said.

"Why am I not in the palace?"

"It's too risky. Too near to the conflict at the tunnel. It wouldn't take much for a sudden reversal to cut off the palace from our forces here," she said.

"I see," Mirella said, nodding her head.

"Laur—" Svella was interrupted as both Inyis and Laurilae rushed on in as well, looking nearly as relieved to see her up as Svella had been.

Nearly, but not quite.

"As I was saying, Your Majesty," Svella started again, grinning a little. "Laurilae proposed an idea. Why don't you tell the Queen about how you saved our asses at the tunnel?"

Laurilae looked bashful, but she stepped forward.

"Well Your Majesty... the elders of the Raven's Guard were preparing a new batch of the concoction for the trebuchets, you see. But I had the idea that... well, what if instead of hurling them at the army at our gates, we instead toted it up over the mouth of the cavern and... well, just dumped it on 'em!"

Inyis laughed, taking great joy in the whole memory of it.

"Yes," Svella said with a nod. "After you passed out, we were pushed back. And for a while it looked like the palace would be cut off from our forces in the city, Your Majesty. But then Laurilae had her idea and we were able to cut off their troops from the tunnel."

"I can't take all the credit," Laurilae said. "Svella commanded the troops that dispatched the Imperial forces that were already in the city, while Inyis personally led some of the women up the mountainside to dump the concoction. Had she been any less deft a mountain climber, we would not have pulled it off."

"I grew up along the mountain slopes, north of here. I know how to scale a cliff," Inyis said with less modesty than Laurilae displayed.

"That's great work, all of you," Mirella said with a smile. "You have done the God-King proud, I am sure."

Svella rose up.

"I realize you're all excited to hear about the Queen's revival, but please. Give her some time now, go back to your duties, we still have a war to win," Svella instructed them all, ushering them away so she could speak more privately with her.

"How bad is it, truly?" Mirella asked, nursing her drink still.

"We are stretched thin, Mirella," Svella said in a soft, weary voice. "We were counting on the new Aristean legion to bolster our forces in the city below, instead we are now fighting on two fronts. Though I have some grave news."

"What is it?" Mirella asked.

"We have lost the city gates. It matters little now, but…" Svella left it unsaid. How would the God-King get in to help them? "The only saving grace is that it seems Annabelle has been out of the picture just as long as you have."

Silence reigned for a while as Mirella looked down into her cup of water.

"Do you know anything about that, Mirella?" Svella asked.

It took her a while to break the silence and answer, but at last she did.

"Annabelle assaulted my mind during the battle. I was taken by surprise, and I think she would have done me worse, but after her spell to clear the tunnel she was clearly weary."

Mirella took a deep breath, letting her shoulders heave before she sighed.

"The rage I felt… the anger." Mirella shook her head, a shiver of disgust travelling through her. "She very nearly destroyed me, Svella. And had she not been so weary, she might have. She's been honing those powers of hers. I can tell. Honing her abilities over others' minds. Or perhaps just mine."

"It was her making you act so… so different," Svella said in realization. All of the strange outbursts, all of the times she'd made comments to the God-King and the women of the coven that she'd never made prior… It had all been Annabelle. The gruesome truth Mirella had been too scared to admit.

Mirella nodded her head.

"She was reaching out across vast distances to try and take back her body at first. Then merely to sabotage me. That reprieve I felt… that brief period where I could lead the city in peace?" Mirella laughed, "She was just too busy manipulating minds on the other side of the mountain to make her way here for her *real* revenge."

They were silent again for a while, but Svella came over, sat beside the Queen and rested her hand upon Mirella's shoulder.

"You fought back and kept control, despite all that. And in spite of the disasters here, you are still Queen of this city," Svella insisted.

"But for how long, old friend? Without the God-King's support, how long can we keep them at bay?" she asked, looking wide-eyed at her friend.

"Not long," Svella answered honestly. "Another week, maybe two at most. By then even if they haven't broken through at the tunnel, they will have taken too much of the city for us to hold onto what's left. Already the citizens are cramped, our resources dwindling."

"We need the God-King. And fast," Mirella said.

CHAPTER 40

Mirella had tried countless times since that first experience, to recreate her visit with the God-King. But each time she failed.

Instead of an opulent palace bedroom this time, she lay down upon a lowly cot in the barracks. A simple bed not unlike the ones she had rested upon for almost all of her life as a servant and slave.

Night was approaching, dusk settling in, but Mirella closed off the shutters and dismissed all her servants. She wanted quiet.

She let it all go, let the worries, the fears, the presence of reality itself melt away… and thought only of him. Her lover. Her mate.

With the coarse fabric of the military cots beneath her, pressing to her smooth, pale skin, she felt more like herself. And no alien consciousness scratched at the surface of her mind.

She was all Mirella then, despite what surface appearances suggested.

It was strange how easily it came then, to how she struggled to find the right mix before. But before she knew it, she no longer lay upon a cot in the barracks. She stood upon the grass in a northern field, far off. She saw the setting sun, then heard the rumble of a great many horses.

She turned and looked, seeing there the Ka'reem army on a steady pace over the grass, preparing to set up camp, it seemed.

The forces took sight of her, though, and began to shift.

A cry went up as the head riders came close and saw it was her.

"The Queen!" they shouted. "It's the Queen!"

She had no idea anyone but Kulav could see her like that, transposed across the vast distances in her gilded armour.

A panic took her heart... did she not see Kulav because he was dead?!

Through all her worries and doubts, she never once, not a single time, let herself think he might have failed. Might have fallen. But for a brief, chilling moment her heart froze... right up until he came riding out from the throng of horses, eyes wide.

"My Queen..." he said, breathless then smiling.

He dismounted and came to her, sweeping her up off her feet as the soldiers watched him spin her about.

"Ohh I have missed you!" he declared shamelessly, and she could not help but put her arms around his neck, cling to him, kiss his glossy black hair and forehead.

"I have longed for you so dearly, your Greatness," she said, tears welling up in her eyes.

He squeezed her tight before finally lowering her down enough to kiss her lips, a grin upon his own face.

"We ride home to you victorious. The Imperial army was utterly annihilated, and we are eager to crush its other wing and free you from their assault," he said in his deep, husky voice.

It broke her heart to put worry into him.

"Time is running out, my love," she said, her smooth, pale brow furrowing. "Disaster upon disaster has struck, the wall crumbled on its own for reasons we know not… the old tunnel was cleared, and troops press in upon us from both ends."

The worry in her own expression was wiped away by the stern seriousness that crossed his face. Kulav became grimly set.

"How long do you have before you can hold out no longer?" he asked in a serious tone of voice.

"A week. Maybe more, but it is unlikely. They have a secret weapon that threatens us, and they have taken the gates," she said, swallowing, anxious about telling him the full story.

"We will ride hard and without rest for as long as we can," he declared loudly so his men could hear around him. "Keep moving! We ride through the night!" he told his men before gesturing to have his horse brought to him.

"We need our God-King," she said, leaning up and kissing his lips sensuously, enjoying the moment. For it would be brief.

He ran his hand along her cheek and back in through her hair before pulling back.

"I shall come to you in but a few nights. I promise you this, my Queen," he said to her, a fiery love in his eyes as he stared into her gaze. "We shall ride hard and be there in time, even if it costs us dearly."

"Ride swift, but ride wisely, my love," she said before a final kiss as he mounted atop his horse.

"Keep the city just awhile longer. We come back to end this siege and send the Empire running. For good this time!" he declared before sending his horse off galloping with the army of riders.

Mirella stared at the back of her lover for as long as she could.

She only hoped that Annabelle wouldn't return with some new heinous new assault before Kulav could make it.

CHAPTER 41

Ariste had transformed so much in just a few short years, and especially so in the past few months.

The once beautiful, intricately laid-out city was now a shambles. Streets and buildings were converted into makeshift fortifications, collapsed structures abounded. It was clear that even once the war was over, a great deal of rebuilding would be necessary to return people's lives back to a semblance of normal.

"It will take at least a few years restore Ariste to its former glory, Your Majesty," Laurilae said, summing up the report for Mirella.

"Isn't it a little premature to be thinking of what comes after the war when we still wage it so desperately?" Inyis asked during their little conference.

"We must always be thinking several steps ahead," Mirella cautioned as she peered out the window. It wasn't the view she had from the palace, but it still let her see much of the city.

"While you both see destruction, I see opportunity," she continued, turning back to them. "It's been four days now since I last heard from the God-King, his arrival is imminent. And with it, victory," she said it with more conviction than she felt. "Once the war is over, we shall rebuild Ariste, but not as it once was."

"Your Majesty?" Laurilae said, looking concerned by that declaration.

Mirella clasped her hands, still wearing her Royal Regalia, armour and pomp combined into one.

"As it is now, the city remains stratified by class. The wealthy of old, though stripped of much of their power and influence, still remain in their posh mansions and estates in the secure upper reaches. While it was the humble homes below near the wall that suffered most," she said, choosing her words carefully.

"That's right, your majesty. But the wealthy families have been bunking with the poorer to make room for our population as they retreat with each fallback," Laurilae said.

"Correct. And while they believe it to be temporary, I feel we should use this opportunity. These people, after all, did not earn their wealth from the sweat of their brows, they inherited it, like they inherited their manors. We should adapt the

Aristeans to a more… Ka'reem way of live," she said with a smile and a nod to Inyis.

"The better homes go to those who earn them," Inyis said, thinking she understood.

"Perhaps," Mirella said, thinking it through. "But if we do that, then the children of the hardest working will then be given an advantage over the others, will they not? And hence we ensure the next generation shall be dominated by the heirs of the last's achievements."

She wet her lips as Inyis spoke up again.

"This is why we Ka'reem prefer to raise our children communally. The clan generally does the bulk of parenting," she said, "barring exceptions of course."

"Precisely," Mirella said. "But I do not think that Aristeans would be so keen to adapt that system so… abruptly. What if, instead, we built more communal homes in the city? And reserve single homes for those who earn them and who are so committed to their profession as to focus solely upon it?"

"To forego parenting for their career?" Laurilae asked.

"Precisely," Mirella said with a smile.

"So we use these manors up here in the higher regions to house those who excel?" Inyis asked, brow arched.

"No," Mirella said firmly. "We convert the manors in the upper reaches into communal homes, care centers and orphanages. War creates orphans, after all, and this has been a long one. Our children need the most care, and should be kept away from danger."

"It won't be easy convincing the wealthy home owners to move from their manors here," Laurilae cautioned.

"True," Mirella said. "But many of those homes were damaged in the assault from the tunnel, or commandeered as fortifications. For the remainder, we could impose a rebuilding tax after the war ends, which they can either pay and hold onto the home until their death — at which time the home passes to the crown rather than their kin — or trade control of their home for a spot reserved in them."

"I like it," Inyis said with a confident smile.

"I am no politician," Laurilae said, "but I think this will take some finesse to pull off."

"Undoubtedly," Mirella said, "but I have some more ideas for th—"

The Queen was cut off as a messenger burst into the room.

"Your Majesty!" she said, breathless.

"What is it?!" Mirella asked, stiffening.

"Another army approaches!" the messenger said, taking a nervous gulp. "It is *not* from the west…"

The west. Where Kulav was expected to come from.

That put a panic into them, because there was no way they could withstand even more forces arrayed against them.

Together they all rushed out the door and onto the rooftop. There, the Queen was handed an eyeglass to peer into the distance, one of Aristean make.

Lifting it to her eye, Mirella peered off in the direction the messenger indicated. There she saw something that chilled her blood.

A massive force of cavalry, and though they looked like they could have been Ka'reem steeds, they were in far too many numbers. It could not be Kulav, who would not have had time to make an approach from the north, and while the direction indicated it was support from their kindred on the steppes, it was far too many to account for their low numbers of elderly and underage fighters.

"What is it?" Mirella muttered in confusion.

The armies moved in slow motion, but one thing soon became clear: the Empire at their doorstep saw it as a threat. Imperial troops not within the city wheeled about to take up defensive positions.

"They're friends?" Laurilae said with confusion.

"They cannot be our people... far too many," Inyis said.

Together they watched as the force of cavalry rode upon the Imperial troops, breaking into two. It was a standard tactic of the Ka'reem, and as expected soon after they began to run circles about the enemy's forces, pelting them with arrows.

"It's our people," Mirella said, betraying just how at one she felt with her adopted people. Even if her change of bodies had meant the feeling wasn't so mutual as it once was.

The second force, however, wavered, and was less disciplined. Its riders wobbled, did not stay as centered, as tightly packed. Which was a shame, as it was the larger of the two by far.

Things seem to go badly, and the larger force was pressed upon.

The Imperial forces took advantage of that and went after it, while also trying to push in upon the smaller forces and hem it in.

It was a disaster.

That is, until a third force appeared out of the west…

"The God-King," Mirella said breathlessly.

The women gasped and watched in shock as Kulav's forces came in for a surprise assault. With the Imperial forces wheeled about to fend off the attack from the north, their flanks were exposed, and Kulav took firm advantage of that. His mounted horsemen crashed into the Empire's side, and sewed disarray into its forces.

"Quick!" Mirella shouted, "Implement the plan!"

Inyis took off running, shouting to subordinates. For while they waited, they were not inactive, and spoke not only of the distant victory they aspired to, but the short term necessities.

"We need to take that gate for him," Mirella murmured.

The battle dragged on seemingly in slow motion, but Mirella watched, biting her nail quite literally as she peered through her eyeglass.

"Was it truly wise to wait until he was this close?" Laurilae asked, fidgeting anxiously.

"We had no choice," Mirella said. "If we took the gate back too soon, we could not hold onto it long enough. We had to try and time it with his action."

Mirella watched the streets below and Kulav in the fields, alternating between the two.

She could see her own Raven's Guard women moving into action. From along the section of the wall they controlled, they climbed its edge, while through the streets they made a more direct assault.

Kulav commanded his forces masterfully in the field, keeping the Empire from reorganizing its forces as he sowed destruction amongst its ranks.

Meanwhile her soldiers tried to pull off a miraculous feat through sheer skill and determination, as even with Kulav's forces, and not counting the Imperial army in the tunnel, they were well outnumbered a few times over.

Kulav pushed towards the front gate, and the Raven's Guard, led personally by Inyis, climbed along the inner wall to take the gate controls by surprise.

"C'mon Inyis… you can do it. You're a climber," Laurilae said, rooting hard for the other woman.

Closer and closer they got, until Inyis and her soldiers were pulling themselves up into the gate towers.

At the last moment they were seen, and arrows fired from Imperial positions below.

Some of the Raven's Guard women fell limply, and a gasp was caught in the throats of Mirella and the women around her. The cries of agony and the sound of arrows hitting stone garnered the attention of the Imperial troops in the tower, who turned their attention from Kulav's forces to the now barely a handful of women who were pulling into their fortification.

It was over.
Just like that.
"Nooo!" Laurilae screamed out in anguish.

CHAPTER 42

"There is no action at the tunnel at least. The concoction is still potent enough to keep them at bay for now," Svella concluded, fresh from commanding the Aristean troops there.

"At least we have that," Mirella echoed the sentiment, slouched into a chair.

"Don't beat yourself up, Mirella," Svella said. "We have limited forces, and without your foresight in preparing the Aristean Guard, we would not have been able to contend with what we have even. It is not your fault that the gate couldn't be taken in time."

It was all true, of course. But that didn't solve any of Mirella's problems.

"The God-King won the battle, but because we couldn't take the gate, he had to retreat and wait," Mirella muttered.

"He can beat the Empire out there, we both know this," Svella reassured.

"Yes, but it will take time. You don't crush a force that large so quickly, not when they now use our own walls against him. There's enough of the Imperial Army inside the city now to keep us pinned in, so that even if he wipes out what's out there, we're still at a deadlock."

Silence reigned in the room until a messenger came with an urgent knock.

"What is it?" Svella asked as Mirella stood up anxiously.

"Pardon, Your Majesty, but we just received word over the wall through raven messenger," she said with a bow.

"And?" Mirella asked, wide-eyed and anxious.

"The God-King reports that scouts from out of the Far East are reporting that another Imperial force is on its way. It will be here in a few days at the earliest," she said. "That's all."

She handed over the encoded note to Svella, who read it over but said nothing else but, "A fourth army... damn them, is there no end to the lives they will throw at us?"

Mirella slumped back down into her chair.

"You are dismissed," she said lightly to the woman.

"What now?" Svella said, though even Mirella could tell it was not a question directed at her.

She had a question all the same.

"Summon the witches. All of them. We are going to make a conjuring," Mirella said, sternness returning to her voice even if it was absent confidence. "We shall do what our kind has always done when times are the darkest: we shall sacrifice for the good of us all."

CHAPTER 43

Mirella strode into the chamber, daring to return to the palace grounds for the mystical act.

Gathered all around were a great number of the witches; women of the Raven Guard with a special gift, and a willingness to sacrifice.

These were the initiated, the ones brought into the deepest fold, secrets of a sort the men of the Ka'reem would never know were theirs to keep.

They all awaited the Queen quietly, even those who had never before seen her sit and take part in ritual with them.

"Thank you all, ladies," Mirella said, seating herself at the tip of the ring before the rest followed suit.

"The God-King has returned, but dire news comes from the east. I have summoned you all here, because we need guidance, and you are the ones to give it," she said, cradling her pregnant belly, trying not to think overlong about the life within her, or the children she already had that saw so little of her due to the duties and necessities of war.

"I ask you now to help me peer into the future. To see what it is that needs to be done to make our illustrious and great God-King reign supreme over all." With that, Mirella simply bowed her head and reached out to take the hands at either side of her.

Peering into the future was not like seeing across distances. It was not even like shaking the foundation of the earth, as they'd done before. Peering into the future was a sacrifice of immense cost. Divination meant defying the nature of existence in a more fundamental way than either of those things.

Yet Mirella would dare.

She focussed herself as the chanting began, prepared herself to do what was necessary. Even if it cost her life, or that of her future child's... she would give anything for Kulav.

Instead of the usual feeling, however, something strange happened. It wasn't a vision of the future, it was a voice. A familiar voice.

"You must act," it said, and though it was distorted as if through a filter, Mirella recognized it... how could she ever forget the voice of Kulav's mother?

"I intend to," Mirella said.

"Do not be swayed," cautioned that motherly voice from beyond death's veil. "If you do not give all you have, all you are, then he shall never be ruler of all."

Mirella's eyes teared up, but she nodded.

"I am willing. I won't let him down," Mirella said.

Suddenly, their surreal talk across life and death was interrupted. Interrupted by a presence that was so strong it could never be ignored by Mirella.

Her eyes flung open and she saw before her — before the whole coven — Kulav. The towering, ebon God-King, there. And judging by the gasps and shocked stares, Mirella did not see him alone.

"God-King!" came the cries from around the room, and Mirella pushed herself to her feet.

But Kulav did not look pleased.

"How did you get here?" Mirella asked in disbelief.

To which he shook his head slowly.

"I know not, my love," he said, his voice gravelly and low. "One moment I was planning my next move, then... I was here. Seeing you about to make a grievous mistake."

Mirella's brows furrowed, and though he took her into his arms, he looked no less displeased.

"What do you mean?" she asked him, leaning at an angle so her pregnant belly would not jab into him.

"You cannot do this. I will not lose you," he said sternly, his thick, muscular arms squeezing her against him so tightly.

Mirella's eyes watered and she shut them to try and stem the flow, but it wasn't working.

"It's our only choice," she said. "If we don't… you will never be truly victorious, and our fight could end here."

Kulav didn't dismiss the other women, he merely lowered himself down upon one knee and held Mirella tightly. One hand cupping her face, the other on her hip, he stared into her glossy eyes with his hard gaze.

"I promised you long ago, that if it all ended in defeat, and you were but a mad woman… I would find a way to crawl back here and claim you once more. That even if shame marked me as history's fool, I would drag you back into the north, claim a dark, cold cave, and make it warm with our passion. I meant it then, and I only mean it all the more now." Kulav's voice was dark, serious.

Passionate.

"My mother sacrificed her mind, and ultimately her life, to make me the ruler of all. It is a sacrifice I never forget, that I never take for granted. But that I never asked for," he said, sliding his hand down along her pregnant belly.

"Yet another of my children grows within you, my love. And I would see you both alive and well. If this war ends in defeat, we Ka'reem shall go back to our old ways, and I shall be leader no longer. Only master of my passion, master of my love. Master of you."

His eyes hardened again and he pressed his forehead to hers.

"You shall make no sacrifice," he said firmly, his voice a husky command. "None of you shall!" he demanded with anger, before cupping Mirella's two cheeks and kissing her hard.

It was a long, passionate embrace but when he broke apart he rose up to his towering height.

"I have a plan, and I shall wrest victory from the jaws of defeat! You have your orders," he said to them all, but to Mirella most emphatically. "Defend this city, hold out. But do not offer yourselves upon any pyre. Enough of my love has been sacrificed for my glory. Far more than enough."

He began to fade from view then and there, as if he were made of fog that faded away with the breeze.

"I am coming for you, my love. And I aim to take you with all the passion and fury of a man turgid with victory. The world will be mine, oh yes. But it will be mine by my design," he declared in a loud, gruff voice before he vanished entirely, leaving the room of women breathless.

CHAPTER 44

Mirella felt a conflicting mixture of emotions after Kulav's visit.

She felt anxious about not playing her full hand, about holding back from the utmost sacrifice, but more than that she was invigorated by his inspiring words. The rough way with which he handled and spoke to her.

He was not a man to be denied.

"The troops are ready, Your Majesty," Svella announced to Mirella. "Are you sure about all this?" she asked in a much softer voice, intended for her ears only. "It is quite a gambit."

Mirella looked hard, harder than she ever had before in that form. She nodded to Svella, clenching her fists.

"We are going to risk it all, just as the God-King himself does. And if we fail, then we did not fail for lack of trying, my friend."

She rose her voice as she stepped out before the forces arrayed around the tunnel.

"The God-King forbids us from merely throwing our lives away in his honour. But he has said nothing against our fighting for him," she declared loudly, striding along the front of them all, in full view of the Imperial troops on the other end, even if the invisible barrier of that pungent concoction separated them.

"But this is a fight I hope to engage in and win. In fact, I plan nothing but," she said boldly. "Let us pray for victory."

Mirella bowed her head, looking so amazingly elegant in her regal armour. It had to be altered to fit her more athletic form over the past few months, but it looked no less glorious for it, and the knicks and scrapes that could not be polished out only added to her magnificence in the eyes of the Ka'reem.

While the Aristeans worshipped versions of the southern deities, the Ka'reem themselves had no gods as such. Only the spirits of their ancestors. And chief among them were declared Saints. Saints such as the God-King's mother.

It was her then, that Mirella reached out to. A force beyond the mortal coil that she knew to be real.

"Please, mother… mother of my love, mother of my fate. You brought me into his service, saw what was to come and nudged us both in the right direction," she said, her heart swelling as she reached out to that woman she only knew in life as a lunatic. A mad woman.

"I know I have not heeded your warning, but if there is one I answer to over you... it is him. And I cannot deny him. Not now," Mirella said within her mind.

"You risk it all. Yourself and your children even, despite what he tells you," came her voice, as real as if it was whispered into her ear, yet as unreal as light out of darkness, stretched thin across the whole of the universe from death unto life.

"I know. Which is why I pray to you for aid... even though I know I have no right to it. You, who gave more than any woman could imagine, who gave all she had... for her son and his glory." Silence. *"Please, help us."*

No more words.

No more advice from beyond the fold.

No sign her prayer was even heard.

Mirella raised her head, a hard gaze upon her face for her soldiers.

"Hold the line. I go and return alone," she declared with full regal power, right before turning and striding through the noxious fumes, untouched, unharmed. Undaunted.

CHAPTER 45

Yvel watched it all from a secluded window in the palace.

The opulent grounds were all but vacant in recent times, considered too much a liability by the Raven's Guard. So she dared something perhaps foolhardy, and brought Adom with her.

"What is she doing?" he asked, muttering into Yvel's ear.

"I have no idea. I heard she was to make her great assault. Her last stand," she replied to the man, cradling her over-full belly, struggling with the weight it caused.

"By herself? No, she must be going to give terms of her surrender," he said.

"I very much doubt it," Yvel said with a snort. "But… we may be able to make the most of this."

Her eyes shifted to his and a devious smirk crossed her lips.

"Once a conflict bursts out, I might be able to stick something in the pretty princess… and end it all here and now, while everything perches upon the razor's edge," she said, flashing a tiny, curved dagger.

Adom looked to it, then to her, then back out the window.

"It's risky," he said, before peering at Yvel again.

"Don't worry, pet," she purred through pouting lips, reaching to touch his chest with consoling hands. "I won't strike until I know it's safe."

CHAPTER 46

Svella led a contingent of Aristean troops on down the battered alleyways of Ariste, down towards the heart of the city and the center of the fighting. It was with grim determination that she moved, a heavy heart and little hope for success, but then a strange thing happened.

She felt a cool breeze coming down from the northern steppes, then a light tickle of a cold snowflake against her skin.

Looking up, she saw thick, grey clouds moving in fast, and a breeze that soon became a harsh wind. The weather was turning dark and dangerous at the hour of decision.

CHAPTER 47

Mirella strode forth down the tunnel. The Imperial troops waited at the other end but she didn't need to go far.

"I know you can hear me," she said, as much in her head as aloud. "I can feel you, like a tickle at the back of my throat. The warning of oncoming sickness," Mirella said.

There came no response at first, but then… there it was. That old, familiar presence, but corrupted. Polluted with anger and hate.

"You are going to pay," came Annabelle's voice.

"Come then. Meet me face to face. Show me your vengeance unsheathed," Mirella said, looking around, seeing no one. Hearing nothing. "I have wronged you. Taken what's yours. Don't you want it back? My troops are well away. Unable to cross the barrier like you or I could," she said to the woman, who still did not answer.

"What did it take to get them to bring you out here anyhow? To trust you enough to do this? What snivelling did you have to do? What begging?" Mirella said, adopting a different tactic, sneering as she said her words. "Did the snotty little stuck up princess have to get on her knees and please a man just to be taken back home, is that it?" she said. "Did she have to debase and sell herself for so flimsy a token?"

Mirella snorted with disgust.

"Did you finally get a taste of what it's like to live a real life? To make hard choices and not have everything handed to you upon a gilded platter?" she asked. "Petulant brat."

Mirella almost turned away in the resurfaced anger at that woman who owned and used her for so long, but then she saw motion at the other end of the tunnel.

The soldiers parted and a lone figure strode out from between them.

"You have no idea what you have awoken in me," came Annabelle's voice.

Just a split second before a mystical force struck Mirella so hard it knocked her from her feet and onto the stone ground, sending her scimitar flying.

CHAPTER 48

The bitter northern wind was something that every Ka'reem was accustomed to. Out upon the steppes there was never a moment of calm. It was not like existence beneath the mountain, where shelter from wind was a normal feature of life. On the steppes, it was a constant series of daggers that dug into your exposed flesh and tested your mettle.

"You all, stay in the streets. You handle the Imperials down here," Svella ordered the Aristeans, relaying commands to the forces beneath her so they set off to carry them out.

Laurilae stood with them.

"You are not a soldier, Laurilae. You are Battle Engineer to the Queen," Svella cautioned.

"I am going," she said obstinately, the stout woman crossing her arms over her chest and showing no signs of standing down.

"Very well," Svella said with only a moment's delay. There was no time to debate, and she let Laurilae and the others head off.

"Raven's Guard," she said sharply to the remaining commanders beneath her. "We face a great enemy that far outnumbers us. But we fear nothing under the skies. And their thick metal armours will not shield them from our rage. Not this day!" she said, filled with venom.

"We go to take back what was and remains ours," she said before climbing the city walls at the far western edge, the last segment that they controlled.

A blast of icy wind and sleet — rain mixed with snow that bit into the skin and froze on contact — struck her, but she was undaunted. She merely peered out over the battlefield beyond, watched as the God-King's forces attacked, retreated, then attacked again in multiple well-coordinated prongs, drawing out the imperials to pursue his horseback forces.

"Where Inyis and our sisters fell, we shall redeem them," she said, brandishing a climbing hook, ready to dangle herself from the wall and attempt the treacherous tactic once more.

CHAPTER 49

Mirella was dazed by the blow, and lost a few seconds before she recouped enough to push Annabelle back out of her mind. But that was again a momentary victory before another assault sent a stab of pain through her mind.

"You took everything from me!" came the shrill cry of Annabelle down the tunnel, the woman still a dark shadow in the distance.

Mirella tried to get up, but was struck once more. A piercing sound, so unnatural and hateful, filled her mind and she stumbled about, only barely able to shield her pregnant belly from harm.

"You betrayed me! You took care of me more than my own mother and father, and you betrayed me!" she bellowed, and with those words came another assault that both deafened and blinded

Mirella to all but the sight of the light at her end of the tunnel.

The greyish white light that slowly took on the form of heavy downfall, ice and freezing-rain pelting her line of troops, the rising cold undoing the noxious fluid that was their only line of defense against Imperial intervention.

Her gambit would be a complete loss the moment the Imperial troops took advantage.

CHAPTER 50

Laurilae was no fighter, but still she accompanied the Aristean troops against the Imperial invaders.

These were her people, the same ones she'd grown up with, passed by on the streets. They were her kin as much as anyone, raised as an orphan as she was.

She had to stand by them.

Though as the heavy ice and sleet fell upon them, noisily clattering off their shields, it felt like a grim march.

They advanced towards the Imperial lines, clad in a mix of leather armour, inlaid with chain and silks similar to that the Ka'reem wore, and the special shiny shields of Aristean make. They were spry, but defended.

The mix of men and women in the Aristean Guard moved forward quickly, and what would've been quietly but for the rattling of hail chunks striking their shields. It ruined their hopes of surprise, Laurilae lamented.

Yet they got in so close without the Imperial's opening fire and forming defensive ranks.

That made her worry more than ever.

She thought to herself that at least worries kept her from dwelling on the cold, but though Aristeans were nowhere near as hearty in the icy weather as the Ka'reem, they were used to winter.

Even if it was a winter that was several months freakishly early and without warning.

On they went, quiet as they could but for the mental *tinks* of ice upon metal, though as they got closer... the noises grew louder, echoing to nearly thunderous heights as they went.

The reason became obvious when Laurilae peered through a busted window of what was once a home, but was now little more than a ragged wall exposed to the elements.

Before her, through the ruined cityscape, hundreds upon hundreds of Imperial soldiers marched, their heavy metal armour the target of large hail stones, producing a rhythm that seemed to knell their doom.

CHAPTER 51

It was a risky, perhaps foolhardy gambit, but they had few options left. And if they waited on the God-King to do it all himself, Ariste might be saved… only to fall to the reinforcements that were fast on their heels.

But knowing that Inyis was caught before, Svella took the chance all the same. Despite not being quite the climber the other woman was.

This time, she opted to take the outside wall, hoping fewer eyes would be there as the God-King raised hell outside in the fields, and the Queen's army inside raised hell within.

She couldn't afford to risk many lives on such an operation, but she took all they could spare. The best climbers she could rouse up, after Inyis's failed attempt resulted in the best of the best all dying or being captured.

The chill arctic wind bit into her flesh, made her long for her raven's cloak, the protective garment left behind so it wouldn't interfere with her climb. On and on she went, thankful for the noise of the out-of-season storm that hid the sounds of their climbing claws.

The archers on the wall weren't active, or in sight that she could see, which could only mean in Svella's mind that they were pelting the Aristean Guard on the other side. A distraction at least.

She crawled further and further along, using the muscles in her arms to bring her nearer to her destination, right beneath the guard tower along the walls. But then it hit her…

She peered down, and through the white flurry of snow and ice, she saw arrows pointed her way.

They were caught.

Just like Inyis.

"Fool me twice…" Svella muttered drily beneath her breath.

CHAPTER 52

Mirella's head still stung as Annabelle's constant assault kept her off-kilter, but despite the psychic blows she managed to scramble to her knees.

After so long, there she was… there 'Mirella' was.

It was like nostalgia, but sickening.

Her old body, but dressed in something that looked gaudy and over the top. Something that was never meant to grace a slave woman's form.

"You were like a mother to me! Family! And you betrayed me!" Annabelle screamed, her voice hoarse as she came at Mirella. "You betrayed me for some filthy, stinking savages! To become some mongrel dog's breeding *bitch*!" she spat the words out she was so enraged at Mirella.

Annabelle was bold, coming out without any guards, dressed like a princess once more despite her form. Mirella could see her clearly, make out her form, her face, her makeup and hairdo even.

"And now... now!" she said, unable to finish her thought as she looked over Mirella in her old body, filled with rage at what she saw. "You turn my beautiful... beautiful body into some disgusting... swine stock breeding bin!" she screamed.

Mirella's head spun, she felt dizzy, but she tried to buy time as she inched away along the ground. Though her side remained so far away...

"How did you do it? How did you manage to get back here?" Mirella asked the woman, who was like a twisted mirror.

"Please!" Annabelle sneered at her. "I am a Princess! Trained to rule! I can negotiate my way out of anything. And besides," she said cockily, still slowly approaching as the psychic assaults continued to strike against Mirella's mind. "One good thing did come from this body switch, my servant... I gained access to powers you were far too sheepish and weak to tap into!"

Mirella watched, amazed at Annabelle's resilience. How she used such powers continually, without exhaustion.

She had assaulted the mountain in her rage, after all. Continuously. Stubbornly. For so very long.

"Please," Mirella said, being stubborn herself. "You could not have gotten this far just with your own trickery. Even your mind games don't go that far!"

"Shut up!" Annabelle screamed, jabbing an arm into the air in Mirella's direction, striking her with another psychic assault.

"Who helped you? Who was it?!" Mirella demanded. "What man did you sell yourself to for this, Annabelle?" she taunted.

"No! No man. No one. Your own people betrayed you for me!" she said, wide-eyed and giddy.

The news shocked Mirella, made her almost hesitate, but not quite.

"You lie! They would never betray me," she said.

Annabelle laughed as she came closer and closer, each step taking her nearer as the cold winds whipped through the tunnel.

"Ohhh, but they did..." she said, almost within reach. "The sweetness of it all is that they think they're being loyal to you. To the whiny little servant girl who won their loyalty. I can't wait to wipe the smug smiles from their faces just like I'm going to beat you into a bloody pulp here and now," Annabelle boasted.

Mirella cringed, looking up at the hateful woman. Seeing her come within range and raise her foot, ready to cruelly stomp Mirella's swollen, pregnant stomach.

CHAPTER 53

Laurilae moved with the soldiers as they charged in against the Imperials. She had no weapons like them, but she did have something.

It was an augmented Imperial crossbow. A mechanical device of her own design, that could fire more arrows in quick succession than any other of its make, armed with Ka'reem arrow tips.

So as the Aristean Guard charged in, spears and shields brandished, she climbed atop a crate and opened fire.

It was hopeless odds, but she was committed. Filled with seething anger after what happened to Inyis. At what was done to her city. At the threat to the new social order which let her become a respected royal consultant, rather than a street rat.

The Imperials were slow to react, though there were so many, they crowded around pathetic, makeshift fires, trying to warm up in the storm. Many of them fell to spears in the back before the battle cry went up, and arrows followed.

As slow to move as they were to react, the southerners — used to a hot, humid climate — were dressed in metal with little else. Their armour was stuck to their flesh, causing pain and making them shiver. And as they attempted to defend themselves, the nimble Aristeans out-fought them.

The numbers were completely mismatched, but for skill and prowess in that environment, the Aristeans felt like peerless warriors.

Laurilae even managed to let fly a crossbow bolt into one of the enemies, though her aim was far from great, and she struck their heavy armour instead of one of the weak points. Suddenly, a curious thing stood out to her.

The chilling cold must have made their metal brittle and weak in the face of the Ka'reem arrow tips, because her tiny bolt pierced the armour far more readily than it should've and sent one man to his grave.

It quickly made sense to Laurilae, and she shouted out.

"Their armour! You can pierce their armour! The cold's made the metal weak!" she cried back to the actual archers, a grin lighting up her face.

CHAPTER 54

Svella faced her death head on, as always.

And as always, it didn't come.

She took the outside of the city walls instead of the inside for two reasons: because she hoped the soldiers there would be more distracted, and because the winds off of the steppes might make targeting them harder.

The second point proved the greatest, because that brutal arctic wind refused the Imperial arrows their targets, and deflected them widely from the women.

Ignoring their assault, Svella carried on, climbing along the wall further and further until they were there. A simple pull and she was up over the side, staring at the back of the Imperial archers as they lobbed arrows into her countrymen and allies.

Before her sisters could even climb up and join them, she was sliding a dagger into one man's back and hurtling him off the wall as he screamed. Another went soon after.

The Imperials were sluggish in the bitter winds and cold, one even slipped upon the icy sheet that covered the floor, and the other Raven's Guard women were there in time to quickly dispatch the archers.

"Clear the barrier! Let our sisters up here!" Svella commanded, women rushing off to take down the Imperial barricades along the wall, letting a rush of fresh Raven's Guard archers through.

"Bow-Sisters! Rain death! The rest, to me! We take the rest of the wall!" Svella declared, bold and haughty, feeling like nothing could stop her.

CHAPTER 55

Annabelle's heeled boot crashed down in time with a psychic assault, her weapon of choice apparently finely honed after so long.

But nearly all the time that Annabelle had spent honing her skills on assault, Mirella had spent honing her defense. And she deflected the psychic attack almost as deftly as she grasped the woman's boot, twisted her ankle and sent her falling to the ground.

"Vanity and ego were always your downfall," Mirella said, spryly standing up, as if her pregnant belly were not an impediment at all.

"How dare y—" Annabelle was cut off as Mirella sprang into action and kicked the woman in the side, making her cry out.

"I dare!" Mirella shouted, grasping the hair that was once hers and yanking Annabelle by it, tossing her into the wall. "I dare for me and all the others born into my life that had to smile and suffer the insufferable! Who had to play maid and nurse to spoiled brats that thought they could own another simply because of the luck of their birth!"

Annabelle lashed out again psychically, rebounding despite the brutal physical lashing, and Mirella couldn't deflect it entirely.

"You betrayed me! There is no greater sin than betrayal!" Annabelle cried out as she took the opportunity to rise back up.

"I agree," Mirella said, wobbling momentarily before she gracefully spun about and kicked her in the side of Annabelle's head. "But it's no betrayal to claim your freedom from a slave master!"

Mirella punched Annabelle in the gut, knocking her back against the stone wall, then hit her across the jaw in quick succession.

"You cannot steal what is stolen! You only right the scales of injustice," Mirella cried back at Annabelle. "You say I was like your kin? Hah! I was your property! I was no more family to you than your expensive dresses," Mirella said, yanking Annabelle forward by her dress to head butt her.

Annabelle, however, struck her with a powerful telekinetic blast that knocked her back, and loosened some of the stones above, sending them crashing around them.

CHAPTER 56

With the Raven's Guard women back on the walls and their arrows piercing the Imperial armour so easily, the tides of battle within the walls were shifting readily.

Laurilae watched as what not long ago seemed a hopeless battle, was instead a rout. The Imperials were dropping their shields and turning, fleeing back towards the breach in the wall, from whence they'd made their first breakthrough.

Her crossbow was empty, and she had to stop, falling behind the other Aristeans as they made their advance to reload. But as she pushed more bolts into the crossbow, she heard a sound through the storm: the cries of women.

Stopping short of her task, she followed after it, hearing familiar voices crying out for help.

In the battered ruins of a home, she saw a stairway leading down into what was once a cellar, and there she heard voices… so familiar.

She had but one crossbow bolt at the ready, but she advanced down with it raised, prepared to fire.

The stairs creaked as she descended, and the voices stilled, but Laurilae persevered, more determination than sense as she went into what could easily be a trap.

It was dark down there, only a small fire for light.

"Who's down here?" she asked, but then an arm reached out to grasp her.

Laurilae tried to resist, but she was no match for the strength behind it. The Imperial man growled at her.

"Fuck off!" Laurilae shouted, but she couldn't overcome him, not even enough to aim the crossbow at him and fire.

But then, from deeper into the cellar, a woman came out. Bound and tied at the wrists and ankles, she didn't so much charge as stumble out, but she propelled herself at the man, knocking him askew, and loosening his grasp.

Laurilae raised her crossbow and fired. She pierced his chest, making him cry out before he fell to his knees in pain, then collapsed into death.

The Aristean woman's heart was pounding, and she was breathing hard, having gotten through that so narrowly. But then she saw who had helped save the day.

"Inyis!" she cried out, dropping her weapon before falling to her knees. She grasped Inyis, helped pull her up before squeezing her in an embrace. "You're alive!" she said.

"Someone has to keep you from getting yourself killed in dark holes," Inyis said drily.

"I thought you had died!" Laurilae said, eyes brimming with tears.

"No. No time for death. Not while there's a war to fight," she said, pushing her arms up. "Now come. Untie me and the rest of us. I know where they are keeping more prisoners. We can get straight into the battle."

Laurilae wiped at her face with the back of her sleeve and nodded.

"Okay. We've got them on the run, we can win this thing," she said so matter-of-factly.

"What?" Inyis said, sounding confused. "The hell has been happening out there that things have turned so quickly?"

"Oh, just a spot of precipitation," said the Aristean engineer.

CHAPTER 57

Svella ran down the ramparts with her sisters at her back. They routed the Imperial arches from the walls with relative ease, her own bow-sisters taking up positions and raining death down upon both sides.

It would normally be a precarious position, but as she peered out over the city and then the fields, she saw that the Empire was on the run, on both sides.

Worse again for them, they both ran into each other.

The troops within the city tried to flee out through the gates, while the Imperials outside being pressed upon by the God-King tried to race into the city to take shelter from the cavalry. The result was a crush of cold metal bodies upon slippery stone and icy earth.

A horn sounded as the commander tried to rally the forces, but the soldiers didn't heed it. It was far too chaotic for that. And worse still for the commander, the freezing soldiers began to throw up their arms in surrender.

First it was a few isolated cases that stuck out amid the throngs, but then Svella started to see that surrender was spreading through their ranks like wildfire.

Out in the fields, the Ka'reem horsemen encircled and cut off the Imperial commander as the God-King's banner-guards swung back towards the walls.

"Get that damn gate up!" Svella shouted back down the wall. "The God-King is coming home at last!"

There was little more down here to do than wrap things up, both Svella and the God-King realized that. But up above…

Mirella gambled with her life.

CHAPTER 58

Annabelle's attack shook the very mountain, loosing stones upon not only Mirella but the Imperial troops that waited just down the tunnel. Death cries went up, but Mirella managed to spring out of the way of the large rocks that threatened to kill or injure her.

Though as Mirella prepared to spring in for another attack, she felt a twinge of pain shoot through her midsection that set her knees to shaking.

"Ahh!" she cried out, realizing that her child-to-be was growing over-eager to be born amid the battle.

"We treated you so well," Annabelle said, rising up, blood running from her nose as she assaulted Mirella again, making her cry out in pain. "Not like other slaves. And you threw it all away to roll in the mud with these... these animals!"

Mirella did her best to take control of her body as she'd been mastering over recent months, to hold off the birth. Though she might control her body, however, the life within her was ready to be born, and her ability to maintain control it weakened.

The pain still wracked her body, but Mirella sprang forward to punch Annabelle in the nose, a sickening crunch meaning she'd be bleeding all the more.

"You don't get it, even after all of this," Mirella said, striking up with her hand against Annabelle's chin, knocking her head back into the wall. "You could have treated me as good as royal kin, though you didn't," Mirella interrupted only to scream as Annabelle hit her with another psychic assault, "but I was still your property! And nothing but the freedom to dictate my own destiny could soothe that!"

Mirella backhanded the woman roughly, sending her toppling to the ground. Annabelle's rage gave her more resilience than Mirella ever could have thought she'd have.

"You traded one owner for another!" Annabelle snarled, knocking Mirella from her feet, then locking her into such mental anguish all she could do was scream. "You only made yourself slave to a man who uses you as a breeding cow."

Annabelle grasped Mirella by her blonde hair, yanking it, pulling her along the ground as she filled Mirella's head with visions of death. Despair.

Of seeing her whole new family, her children, Kulav, dying... suffering... pathetic... weak...

The pain that went with those images made it impossible for her to fend off the assault quickly.

Annabelle dared to drag Mirella in front of her own troops, who stared in horror at the sight of their bloodied Queen screaming in agony and mental torture. She pulled a small dagger from her calf and brandished it as the line of Aristean guards watched. They were helpless, for if they approached it'd all be over anyhow.

"Betrayal has a price!" Annabelle screamed before plunging the dagger at Mirella's chest.

Mirella screamed out, the sound of her cry piercing the air as she reached up, took hold of Annabelle's hand and deflected her blow, plunging the dagger into her former-owner's thigh.

Pain still wracked Mirella, her water broken in the icy cold temperature, making her all the more freezing, but she kept herself together enough to twist that blade into Annabelle's leg and use it to pull herself up and push the woman down.

"Love found me, and I chose it," Mirella said as she climbed atop Annabelle and pummeled her face. "You could never understand what it means to someone like me to given the choice in who they love!"

Her face was a bloody mess, splattered upon Mirella's fists long after Annabelle passed out. Though finally, Mirella had all she could take, and toppled to the side, clutching her pregnant belly with her bloodied hands.

"Ahhh!" she cried out as her soldiers marched forward and past her down the tunnel, protecting her from the Imperials, a pair staying behind to help her. They tried to move her, but she couldn't bear it.

"Get a midwife, a healer, someone!" Mirella screamed as the pain stabbed through her.

"Yes, Your Majesty," one woman said, rushing off, leaving Mirella alone with her handmaiden, Yvel.

Mirella's face was covered in sweat despite the icy cold, and her eyelids shut as she panted. She was in pain from the fight as well as the impending birth, exhausted, weary.

"Your pain will all be over soon," Yvel said to the Queen slipping forth her dagger.

CHAPTER 59

Yvel was slow, methodical. Fast movements drew attention quicker than slow ones, she knew. She was a trained fighter, after all. A Ka'reem.

It was a glorious few moments when it seemed that revenge for betrayal would be had, but now Yvel had to do it for her.

Adom came up quietly, for there were soldiers left. The Queen had gambled heavily on this duel, sending all but a handful of guards to leave the impression of a defense at the tunnel, while everyone else she threw into the city below.

"I admire you in many ways, Your Majesty," Yvel said calmly, letting no stray notes of loathing betray her intent as she nodded toward the unconscious woman, indicating for Adom to take her. Her diligent man scooped her up, propping her beneath his shoulder as he moved on ahead, intent upon sneaking through the thin line of Aristean guards.

"You are a cunning woman. A true ruler." The negatives went unsaid as Yvel raised her hand to plunge the dagger into the Queen's heart.

The Queen's chest was heaving, her breathing reduced to panting as she struggled with the pain in her body. But her eyes were shut as she focussed upon the excruciating act of giving birth to yet another of Kulav's children.

She didn't see the dagger coming, her world was a blur of pain, sweat and tears.

CHAPTER 60

Mirella opened her eyes, but she was too weak, weary and shaken with pain to react. She stayed conscious just long enough to see Kulav ride up atop his black stallion, spear in hand. The God-King triumphant.

She didn't even see the dagger held over her, unaware of the threat. Not that there was a single thing she could have done about it.

CHAPTER 61

Yvel cried out in agony as the God-King's spear lanced into her calf, his galloping approach thundering over the noise of her pained scream.

Her dagger-hand clutched at the stone wall as she teetered, but she rebounded to try again. She was caught, but it was too late. She would give her life to exact vengeance, because her life was forfeit already.

She screamed and braced through the pain to stab at the Queen, but the God-King was upon her.

Still atop his horse, he grasped her by the ponytail and pulled her off of Mirella. The dagger clattered to the stonework as he dragged her away from his wife.

The other guard came rushing up with support in tow, the healers gasping at the sight before them.

"Tend to my wife!" he commanded them as he swung down from his steed and bound Yvel.

Yvel seethed, but more than that… she felt panic lance through her as in the commotion, her own birthing began. She let loose a scream as she lay there, set to give birth alongside her most hated foe.

Soralin, the healer, looked between the Queen and Yvel.

"Your Majesty, she's giving birth, too," said the healer, gazing up at the towering God-King.

Kulav barely spared Yvel a glare as he went to Mirella's side, to stroke her hair and kiss her clammy forehead.

"Your Greatness! We can't let her go untended," Soralin pleaded again as the other two healers furiously tended to Mirella.

"Fine! See to her," the God-King relented as Yvel grunted and struggled.

"But do not loosen her bindings. She shall not be going anywhere," Kulav stated as reinforcements rode up to the tunnel.

"Your command, God-King?" asked the commander atop his horse.

Kulav had to struggle to spare the matters of war even a glance, but one look down the tunnel showed that the handful of Aristean guards would not be enough to keep an Imperial army at bay as they already struggled to apprehend the fleeing Adom and Annabelle.

CHAPTER 62

Mirella could feel Kulav grinding his teeth even through her agony; he was struggling with his decision. He wanted more than anything to stay with her.

"Go," she said weakly, reaching out and grasping his hand with hers. "They need you to command them."

"They can charge down there without me," Kulav declared in a gravelly voice, so certain.

"But can they turn defeat into a victory like the God-King can?" Mirella said with a faint hint of a smile on her clammy face. "Go, my love. There will be many more childbirths to come," she assuaged him.

Kulav kissed her once more before rising up.

"See to it that she is taken care of," he commanded before taking the reins of his steed once more and climbing up.

"I shall find a healthy new child, held in my wife's loving arms when I return a victor thrice over," he cautioned them all before sending his horse galloping down the tunnel, his elite bannermen behind him.

CHAPTER 63

Mirella lounged in bed, because for all of her newfound ability to control her body on a level others could not begin to fathom, she had still nearly split herself in twain to give birth to a child of Kulav once more. A few days of relaxation seemed reasonable to her.

"The other side of the mountain is ours, Your Majesty. Its farms and orchards will once again produce fruit and vegetables for Ariste," Svella said with a confident smile.

"If we can hold it," added Inyis.

"Don't be so negative," Laurilae said with a smirk. "We have more than bloodied the Empire's nose this time. We have ravaged most of their army, which must have left their frontiers sorely undefended."

"If they aren't facing challenges all across their realms as a result of this, then I will eat a second tunnel through the mountain myself," Svella boasted confidently.

Mirella let them all talk, smiling lazily as she cradled her newborn daughter in her arms.

"It'll be so great to eat fresh fruit again, oh how I've missed it," Laurilae said excitedly.

"Sounds too fancy for me," Inyis responded, smiling wryly. "Some honey biscuits suit me fine as a snack."

They bantered back and forth, though the sound of loud soldiers' footsteps thundered down the hall outside, gradually interrupting their chat.

The doors flung open as the God-King entered into the room, fresh from meeting the army out of the east after he cleared the tunnel and took the southern slopes of the mountain.

His armour was nicked, scratched, and dented, but he was well and whole, his hair tousled, his face lit with a bright grin.

"My love!" he declared, rushing to Mirella's bedside, leaning one knee upon it as he brought his arms around both her and his new daughter.

Mirella's heart swelled and she pressed into his embrace.

"You're back so soon!" she declared, her voice soft and light as she nuzzled into the crook of his neck.

The God-King kissed her deeply, passionately, unconcerned with all the eyes that watched them in the lavish bedroom.

Kulav took his sweet time getting around to speaking, stroking her blonde hair instead, kissing her, revelling in the feel of her smooth, soft skin.

"The army from the east," he began to speak in between smacks of their lips, "was conscripted from conquered slaves. Told that if they fought us, they would earn their freedom." Kulav finally managed to steal his eyes from Mirella's, to gaze down at their daughter. "I told them that they are already free as far as I am concerned, and may take residence without our lands. And if they chose to fight for us, we would free their homeland and return it to them."

Everyone in the room was struck silent by the news.

"How many joined?" Mirella asked breathlessly, staring at her husband. Her lover.

"Enough to double our numbers," he said with a wry smile.

Everyone broke into jubilant grins, and Laurilae embraced Inyis.

"The Empire is finished," Mirella said with finality.

CHAPTER 64

Ariste was still battered; a month was not nearly long enough to do all the repairs needed, after all. But it looked beautiful as the sun shone down upon its gleaming white stones.

Mirella savoured the moment, the new banners flying, the throngs of people out in force to celebrate Kulav and her victory.

She strode down the palace stairs and out onto the dais where the God-King awaited her. The crowds burst into cheers as she stepped into the bright light, the cool breeze wafting through her cloak.

It had been years since she wore the raven's feathers of the God-King's chosen, not since their marriage, but it suited her so perfectly, still. It reminded her of who she was.

Gone was her round, pregnant belly. Her tummy was taut and firm, just like the rest of her now. She felt confidence and power like never before. Master of herself, in ways others could not even fathom.

She wore traditional Ka'reem garb from head to toe, except for her golden Aristean crown that marked her as Queen.

The God-King looked serious and mighty as he reached out, took her hand, and guided her alongside of him.

"Today," he began, his voice booming out over the city so loudly, "we celebrate numerous victories. Many armies were crushed beneath our might, my people. But more than that, we celebrate a victory over an idea. We have defeated oppression itself as we crushed the might of the Imperial dogs!"

The people broke into thunderous cheers and applause, the mix of Ka'reem, Aristean, and southern free-peoples all jubilant.

"The end of tyrants is nigh!" he declared, taking the crown from Mirella's head and tossing it to the ground as if it were mere trash.

Mirella kept steady, unflinching, unblinking. The crowd went silent.

"The end of slavery, the end of oppression!" Kulav stomped upon the crown, his heavy bootfall twisting, bending and breaking the ancient bejewelled symbol.

"From this day forward," Mirella said, looking up at her husband as her golden hair blew in the breeze, then out over the people around them.

"We shall make it our goal to put an end to Kings and Queens, Emperors and Empresses, Princes and Princesses!" Kulav bellowed.

"To the slave masters and traders, to all who would enslave, oppress or bind others… to all who would claim authority over persons based solely upon their birth!" Mirella shook her head, letting her hair go free from out under the weight of the crown.

"I am God-King no more," Kulav announced in his booming voice, and gasps filled the air.

"But we are your Warlords," Mirella said loudly, "and we shall command for as long as one scrap of land remains upon earth where people remain slaves."

"We shall be the harbingers of revolution and unity!" Kulav added, and Mirella smiled up at him, proud of her husband.

"Until all are one beneath the Great Skies, and the good of all is the sole purpose of state and rulers," she added. "To the end of tyrants great and small!" she cried out as Kulav and she raised their hands together into the air as true partners.

As living equals before the ecstatic crowd, that cheered, shouted, threw confetti and jumped with joy. Before their trusted friends and advisors who gazed on with awe and applause of their own.

EPILOGUE

The palace was bustling, which was not uncommon. What made the current bustle different was the nature of it.

All about guards and staff rushed to pack away and cart off items, what remained of the opulent furniture and ancient vases and decorations. Most of it was simply being moved around, but some was going to fuel the public coffers.

"I can't believe you're doing it," Laurilae said, mouth agape as she watched the people work to repurposing the palace.

"It needs to be done," Mirella said, still wearing the raven's garb that was her new suit of state. "There is no place for a royal palace in the new Ariste. And this will set an example for the former nobles, who are asked to sacrifice their estates or wealth."

"But a school?" Svella said, sounding dubious of the whole thing. "A giant school? Why?"

"It will be the largest academy in the world," Laurilae said with appreciative awe.

"Academy and museum. Open to all. A fitting use for what was once a monument to decadence and oppression," Mirella said, peering around the ancient halls she had worked at as indentured servant for so very long.

"Where will you be staying, though?" Laurilae asked, brow furrowed.

"Are you kidding? She won't be needing a home any time soon," Inyis said with a grin.

"What do you mean?" Laurilae asked.

"Your Warlords are going on the march," Mirella said proudly, hands upon her hips. "A grand tent upon the ground as we ride south shall be my home."

"Who will be in charge of the city while you're away though?" Laurilae asked, brow furrowed.

"I shall command the army in defense of Ariste and the northern steppes," Svella declared modestly.

"But what about the civilian side of things?" Laurilae prodded.

Nobody answered immediately as Mirella grinned.

"How would you two like that responsibility?" she asked Inyis and Laurilae squarely, the two women going wide-eyed and gape-jawed.

"Us?" Laurilae said.

"The both of us?" Inyis asked.

"Right," Mirella nodded. "We have a mixed city now, with people from all over. The civilian administration should reflect that. And you two are able administrators who know how to work together."

Inyis and Laurilae looked at each other, thinking it over.

"We shall think about it," said Inyis, at almost the exact same time Laurilae said "We'll think about it."

Laughter broke out and the women began to chat and discuss the rapid changes, but Mirella had business to get to.

"Excuse me," she said, brushing away, heading back for the King and Queen's bedroom, while it still remained that.

It was one of the last places to be packed up and Mirella had received word that Kulav wished to meet her there.

Though the moment she stepped through the doors, they slammed shut and she was grabbed from behind, arms holding her in place.

"Just couldn't help yourself, huh?" said the dark voice as that strong grasp held her tightly in place.

"You're just too irresistible," she said, enjoying the feel of her husband's thick, corded muscles pressing against her. Then the feel of his full, moist lips kissing along her neck.

"Will you miss this place over the coming years?" he asked her, his voice low and gravelly with desire. Already she could feel that familiar sensation of his manhood pressing into her rear, his insatiable desire for her never far behind.

"Not at all," she said, fluttering her lashes nearly shut as she gave a gentle moan at his kissing, at the way his hands roamed over her body, feeling her with such intense desire, grasping her breast through her leather top. "It was too soft for me."

"The hard ground will solve that," he said with a grin, nibbling her ear as one of his hands slipped into her leather trousers, down over her smooth, pale mons.

She bit down into her plush lower lip, but then abruptly her leanly muscled form snapped into action. She twisted about and freed herself from his grasp, looking up at him with mischief in her eyes.

"We are equals now, remember," she said, an impish playfulness in her voice.

He gave a low growl, that beast of a man coming at her, grabbing for her. She sprung away, her spry step keeping her out of his grasp. She dodged the next one too, but it was a feint, and he caught her in his thick, muscular arms, lifting her up off the ground.

"Got you," he declared, throwing her down onto the bed with him atop her, kissing and nibbling at her neck as his bare chest pressed upon her.

She laughed, and for the first time in what felt like so long, she was truly herself. Her arms wrapped around him, his weight boring down on her, keeping her pinned to him. She threw her head back as she wriggled beneath him, not content to give up their game.

Mirella had used her newfound powers to heighten her physical prowess to unimagined heights, but Kulav remained a man of impressive strength and skill. Her firm body moved beneath his, causing their bodies to grind, his manhood to swell and rub against her form.

But amid his assault of kisses and bites, she managed to get her legs up around him, using her strong thighs to turn the tables and flip them around. She used his bulk against him, so that she managed to climb atop him, trying to pin him down as he looked up with a fire in his eyes.

"You've become such a fighter, a fiery spirit," he said with a husky growl of approval, peering down over her agile body, clad in the raven feathered garb of a Warlord.

There was such heat that grew within her at his words, as if he were calling forth her fiery spirit indeed. She looked down upon him, licking her lips fiendishly as her thighs pressed to his hips, her ass resting atop his impressive package.

"You've always encouraged me to grow beyond the cage that tried to hold me," she purred before her mouth crushed against his, her hips rocking against his throbbing girth.

Their lips were locked, and Kulav grabbed for her, his two big, strong hands grasping her hips and waist so tight. But he didn't move to throw her off again, nor even inhibit her actions. He groaned into her mouth as she ground atop his manhood, making it swell to such obscene proportions.

Though she had grown in her own strengths, both of them knew that she was only atop him by his allowance. Had he decided to shrug her off, it would be only too easy.

They were two rough, rugged lovers, like any other Ka'reem might rut in the northern steppes. His hands squeezed and roamed over her pale flesh, and he nipped at her lower lip, tugged it in his enthusiasm.

They knew it was a game, one last power play beneath the trappings of wealth.

No longer King and Queen, yet they were still surrounded by the opulence that they would soon sacrifice. Their moods had already begun to shift for the more hardened life, and when he nipped her lower lip, she bit back in return.

Her hands roamed along his strong arms, feeling over the lines of his muscles with such relish. When her palms rested against the back of his hands, she moved them back around her so that he was gripping her ass, just as she desired.

Just as he wanted. His fingers dug in and he growled animalistically, watching and waiting for his dainty wife to give in to their matched lusts.

Mirella's new warlord regalia was skimpier than her Aristean finery, a skirt with a slit down one side, and nothing beneath. It was her thick, raven cloak that was to keep her warm, but his hands were in beneath both, and he grasped at her bare ass cheeks, molded those firm cheeks to his lusty hands.

Kulav ground up against her in time to her rocking motions, their loins separated only by his leather trousers. And he was about ready to burst through them.

She loved those moments of desire before they all bubbled over. Part of her wanted to linger longer, to hold onto the sensation just a little more, but she couldn't bare it. She needed him just as he needed her, and she shimmied backwards towards his thighs.

Before he could protest or bring her nearer, her hands found the front of his pants, unfastening them. She reached in, finding that girth, and her eyes fluttered with pure bliss.

Her husband, her partner, was so stiff. His turgid length so hefty and full, it pulsated with bulging veins each time his desires panged through him, from base to that thick, dark, flared crown of his, which leaked precum in his excitement for her.

"Campaigning away from you has been so trying," he said in his husky voice, sliding his hands back up over her form, squeezing her full breasts from either side. "The long, lonesome nights without my one true love…" he said, letting the sentence trail off with the feelings of lonesomeness and longing so apparent upon his heaving breaths.

It was something they both knew so intimately and yet had hardly spoken on to the same depths of his words. Mirella looked down at the ebon shaft in her dainty hands, and felt that urge to lower her mouth and pay worship to it.

But she resisted, instead shifting forward. She let him go, watching him throb atop his stomach as she shimmied towards it, pressing her cunny against his pillar and luxuriating in the sensation.

He raised his brow in surprise, and then acceptance as their two loins pressed together. Her slick, heated cunt was atop his hard, throbbing shaft, and he moaned from the contact, his manhood pulsating in such quick succession. If he was disappointed by her lack of worshipful attention, he didn't show it.

Instead, he squeezed her breasts, then let his right hand roam down over her body, to grasp her ass once more.

Pushing himself up by the strength of his powerful ab muscles, his physique rippled and he kissed her aggressively. He didn't push her off or take back full control, but he rose up enough to force that kiss and taste her sweet lips.

He let her stay on top of him, but his brutal hands dug into her flesh, tormenting her heightened nerves with tingles of pain and pleasure. Even as she took control, he was the one with the power over her.

Her softer groan teased against his tongue and she lifted herself off him just enough to let him spring up from off his stomach. She was teasing herself no less than him, but she was growing greedy. She couldn't wait much longer.

Her tongue lashed against his and the kiss felt nearly bruising, her desires mounting so quickly.

Kulav growled, and he grasped her ass so tightly, his fingers sank into her fleshy, taut rear and lifted her up. His glistening, honey-coated cock throbbed upwards and he attempted to use his raw strength to pull her into place and impale her upon his ebon shaft.

That sheer power of his was something she couldn't outdo in kind. Even her newfound abilities hadn't gifted her with strength to take on his hulking, muscular form. But she was lithe and agile and knew she could squirm out of his grasp, resist the plunge around his manhood that he needed so deeply.

Yet she wasn't just fighting his strength, but her own needs as well, and so though she resisted just long enough to show him she could, she slammed down upon him quick. With their combined efforts, it nearly rendered her breathless, and her eyes squeezed shut as a momentary pain passed through her.

Kulav's girth was so immense, and even after birthing him several children already, her cunt had to stretch so wide to accommodate his impressive cock. She gasped and shuddered atop him, while beneath his muscular body twitched.

He clung onto her tighter than ever, his fingers sinking into her ass, then the other hand working up to get in beneath her harness to grasp her bare, pale tit beneath. He groped that mound with such a raw need, and his shaft pulsated within her. It stretched her canal with each new throb and he lunged for her lips again. He made her take it, punished her for thinking that she could handle him like a pet.

He thrust up into her, another stab of pain striking through her, yet it was torment and torture and bliss all at once.

Despite his harsh actions and his tight grip, though, his words were honeyed. "You are the only one for me," he growled between rough kisses. "You are the woman of my deepest fantasies. The woman I dared not dream even existed, lest the hopeful delusion sour the reality of my waking life."

All of that jealousy that wasn't her, but Annabelle warping her emotions, seemed like a strange nightmare that she could no longer make sense of. She felt his words, knew them to be true, down to her very core.

Her mouth pressed against his harder in reward for the sweet truths he uttered, and her hips rose up, only to slam down upon him once more. It caused her to gasp against his tongue, but it didn't hinder her. If she were to be his equal, then she'd show him that he was her equal in carnal matters as well.

Her pink slit, as little as it was, managed to swallow that immense shaft, time and again as she rode atop him. The straps that held her top in place loosened, and her firm, pale breasts bounced and jiggled as she took him in.

Kulav's hungering mouth wandered from her lips, nipping and suckling down her neck as he moaned, each pump of her slick sleeve around his throbbing shaft making his flesh light afire with pleasure. He squeezed her ass tighter, even dared tweak her stiff, pink nipple between his thumb and forefinger.

Try as she might, she couldn't deny that those little reminders of pain and pleasure twisting into one excited her. That she didn't yearn for it the same way she yearned to feel him throb against her.

But she was in control, and as that sharp pinch made her shudder, she swatted his hand away.

"Gentle," she growled against his mouth, but her kiss was anything but.

The mighty Kulav, once-God-King, now husband and partner alone in their tryst, couldn't be so easily tamed despite his public face.

It was nature to him, something so difficult to contain when she rode atop his dick, and her flesh felt so delightful to his hardened hands. Kulav gave a low, guttural groan and he sucked and kissed at her pale, slender neck, his growling voice so dark.

"I need you," was all he got out.

His words reverberated through her, spoke to her very soul, and she rode him a bit faster, her silky thighs pressed into his hips to hold herself in place. To have that control that she'd never dared to take in all their years together.

"You have me," she murmured against his flesh, peppering his jaw with kisses. "You have every part of me."

Her declaration only made him grasp onto her harder, all that power within his muscular frame held in quivering check by his sheer will. Her rewarding pace increase made him moan a little louder though, and he forced his hands to loosen their hold and stroke over her taut flesh.

His hard, strong hands paid homage to every part of her, her pale physique the absolute epitome of femininity, grace and athleticism. She was more Ka'reem than Aristean now, but more than either, she was simply herself. And she could feel in his every action and word, that she was what he truly wanted. Not an ideal to live up to, but Mirella, pure and raw. As she wished to be.

She pulled away from him, instead letting him look over her semi-clothed body, over the lines and shapes of her raven garb. Her blonde hair tumbled over her shoulders as her spine arched, her hips grinding each time she neared the hilt of his cock.

She grabbed onto his thighs, her body moving to give him a wholly unique experience.

It worked, because Kulav was transfixed.

The Mighty God-King brought to stare upon her gloriously nude form, almost as if he were seeing a woman sexually for the first time. She was unique and profoundly special to him.

His dark gaze travelled over her, soaked in the view of her agile form moving, her pink cunny lips stretched to accommodate his thick, dark girth until it was nearly made red from the strain. Yet again and again she rocked upon him, took him in deep, made him moan lewdly.

He pawed at her skin, her breasts, over her taut tummy, grunting as his dick pulsated with need.

"If I am the Demon Spawn as they say," he managed in deep, breathy words, "then truly you are the body of heavenly bliss itself."

His words sent a shiver down her spine. She'd never thought of him in such terms. To her, he had always been her God-King. Yet as she bit down on her lower lip to keep from screaming, she couldn't help but speed up. To let her body bob atop him more urgently.

"Kulav," she gasped, her palm finding his roaming hand and stroking it affectionately with her agile fingers. "You are my world."

Her quickened pace made him struggle to keep his eyes upon her, the once God-King brought to shuddering bliss as his own climax approached.

Though as the broad, muscular man reached his free hand towards her cunt, travelling along her thigh to her pink petals, he sought to bring her with him.

That dark thumb rubbing around her clit, teasing its edges as he moaned and his pecs tensed before her eyes.

"My love," he growled out.

"My God," she shuddered in return. She'd been so focused on bringing him to pleasure that she'd not realized how close she was to her own brink. That delicious shiver of delight traveled her spine as her blue eyes gazed down upon him.

So much about them had changed. She'd thrown off the shackles of slavery to instead worship a being that was more God than man. Her body was one she wasn't born into, and she'd even been blessed with children.

And he... he'd found something in her he didn't know he wanted or needed, and that had brought out a part of him that no one truly could understand. The direction of his life had shifted course entirely along with his change in values and desires, and with it, the culture of an entire people.

They'd grown together into something greater than the sum of two parts, and when her orgasm coursed through her, she felt closer to him than ever.

She could feel it all on a level she never could before. How the pleasure crackled and burned through her nerves and veins, how it set her aflame. She could feel her body gush her honey slickness over his loins, and feel him tense and lose all control along with him.

It was all so familiar, yet so different.

A new intensity as she lost herself to her pleasure and felt him spill into her. Thick gouts of his seed shooting forth from his stiff cock, pouring from that spasming shaft as he bucked and cried out in pleasure.

She could feel it all on levels unknowable by others. Could feel every virile shot of his seed, seeking to plant itself within her fertile, waiting womb. She felt it all so intensely, more than a normal woman could have… more than she could have but a few years before. And more than that, she felt one with him more intimately than ever. As if his pleasure were also hers, with each pulse of need that sent another thick stream of cum into her.

The intensity would've put her at risk of blacking out just months prior, but instead, it sent a shock of awareness through her that made her more alert than ever. She pressed her hand down onto his chest, the beating of his heart racing through her.

She shuddered as he bucked into her cunny, unable to help himself in the throes of pleasure, and every throb of his veins sent another thrill through her.

It was a high unlike any other of her life, and she milked from him every spurt, every droplet of his seed. She worked his cock within her body as if they were both one and the same, and the bulky, muscular Kulav strained and clutched onto her so tightly as she did to him, as if they were each other's life raft in a tumultuous sea.

It was a long, intense moment of pleasure, that only ended when they were both sweaty, glistening and panting. Their loins spent together, as they sagged, but their hands refused to leave one another.

She lay atop him, the rhythm of their hearts creating a melody that was at once frenzied and sweet, and her head moved into the crook of his neck. She smelled the fresh salt of his sweat mingling with the smell of their combined orgasms, and to her, it was the sweetest scent in the world.

Kulav held her close, his large hands lazily stroking over her body as the last remaining tingles of their pleasure coursed through them.

"Together, my love… we will conquer and unite the world, or else go down in infamy trying," he said in a final husk, kissing beneath her ear before making his way back to her pouty lips.

She made a sound of pleasure against him, her eyes fluttering closed as the rush began to fade, leaving her with a sense of peace and serenity.

"It's a shame that my true name is tarnished. Those of the coven that rebelled against their Queen did so only to celebrate Mirella. Her accomplishments that I can no longer take credit for. They saw me as the usurper to her power, not realizing…" she said with a little bit of sorrow edging into her voice.

Kulav stroked her hair and kissed her lips, quieting her for just a moment.

"We shall set the history right, my love. You have earned the people's trust twice over, and then some. You cast off the royal claim to the throne. We shall tell them the truth of all, let the bards and story-weavers tell the tale. And the people shall judge us fairly," he said in his gravelly, post-coital voice, love still filling his eyes.

Her fingers stroked along his chest, tracing his muscles and feeling the sinew beneath his skin. Her blue eyes found his and her body softened with affection.

She trusted in his judgment in all things, and gave him a soft kiss in reward for his faith in them both.

Theirs was a short reign, yet the flame they kindled in the world surpassed that of the bedroom. Even as they kissed passionately once more in their after-lusts, the fires of their ambition were fast spiralling higher, and a long joint life as conquerors, liberators and lovers lay before them.

He grinned up at her soft kiss, deviousness sparking in his eyes. He wasn't done with her. Not by a long shot. In a swift motion he pinned her in place as he flipped her onto her back, looming over her with a wicked grin.

"My turn," he growled before sealing her lips in a bruising kiss.

NOTE FROM THE AUTHORS

Thank you so much for reading and purchasing our story! You can check out the rest of our catalogue at http://jmkeep.com.

Did you enjoy yourself? Take a quick second to tell your friends in a review on Amazon and Goodreads! Reviews are a great way of helping other readers to find our work and make it so we can write more frequently!

We love connecting with our fans! You can find us here:

Website: http://jmkeep.com/

Twitter: @jmkeep | @jekeep

Facebook: http://www.facebook.com/jmkeep

Remember, though. The best way to find out what major projects we have in the work is through our newsletter at http://jmkeep.com/newsletter! You'll get a free book just as a thanks for signing up.

MORE BY J.E. & M. KEEP

Novels:
The Vixen Torn
The Vixen Arises
The Vixen Triumphant
Theodora's Descent
Magic Academy
When Dreamers Wake
Chanting the Ancient Lay
The Warlord's Concubine
The Mistress
Vile Wasteland
Forgotten Thrones

Erotic Novellas:
In Her Dreams
Brutal Passions
Bound as the World Burns
Her Master's Madness
Her Master's Corruption
Outcast
Outcast 2: Her Survival

BIOGRAPHY

Joshua and Michelle Keep combine fantasy, sci-fi, horror, romance and mystery into exciting and titillating books.

As long term, loving partners in a very happy relationship, they love to torture their characters. Dark romance wraps its way around all of their stories, corrupting both characters and readers alike.

Some of their work contains dubious consent and erotic pain, so it's not for the faint of heart. Their stories are often called twisted and arousing — at the same time.

Joshua and Michelle have been writing fantasy erotica for over 10 years from their home in St. John's, Newfoundland Canada. They are the owners of Darknest Fantasy Erotica, a forum dedicated to adult fantasy and video games.

Newsletter: http://jmkeep.com/newsletter
Patreon: http://www.patreon.com/jmkeep
Facebook: http://www.facebook.com/jmkeep
Youtube:
http://www.youtube.com/user/JMKeepSFF/videos
Twitter: http://twitter.com/jmkeep |
http://twitter.com/jekeep
Email: admin [at] jmkeep [dot] com